SIERRA HIGH

Once Buck Drayton gives his word, it is kept. So when old J. D. Daniels sends him to Wyoming to recover the body of his son and locate the man who had cared for him, Buck intends to do exactly that. However, someone else has other ideas, and Buck encounters ambushes, fights, a 'widow' who acts like a good-time girl, and a gambler who aims to exploit the situation. But Buck intends to keep his word — even at the cost of his life, or of the lives of those who stand in his way.

Books by Jake Douglas
in the Linford Western Library:

LAREDO'S LAND
RIO GRINGO
RIO REPRISAL
QUICK ON THE TRIGGER
A CORNER OF BOOT HILL
POINT OF NO RETURN
SUNDOWN

JAKE DOUGLAS

SIERRA HIGH

Complete and Unabridged

LINFORD
Leicester

First published in Great Britain in 2000 by
Robert Hale Limited
London

First Linford Edition
published 2002
by arrangement with
Robert Hale Limited
London

British Library CIP Data

Douglas, Jake
   Sierra High.—Large print ed.—
   Linford western library
   1. Western stories
   2. Large type books
   I. Title
   823.9'14 [F]

   ISBN 0–7089–9764–3

Published by   F
F. A. Thorpe (Publishing)
Anstey, Leicestershire

Set by Words & Graphics Ltd.
Anstey, Leicestershire
Printed and bound in Great Britain by
T. J. International Ltd., Padstow, Cornwall

This book is printed on acid-free paper

1

Trust

Because of the rain washing out the tracks, it had taken Buck Drayton five full days to trail the rustlers to their hidden canyon.

He heard the cattle bawling first and this was what led him to the narrow entrance that had been covered with cut brush. It was just on sundown and the shadows were long and Drayton went in low with Winchester loaded, thumb on the hammer spur, and six-gun loosened in his holster. He had guessed at three riders and when he stretched out behind a small juniper that was how many he counted moving about the crude shack built a little way back from the stream. The cows were grazing peacefully on a patch of grass and as far as he could tell all twenty-three were there. The men were cooking outdoors over a fire that smoked profusely because of damp wood.

They had apparently shot some animal, a goat or a deer it looked like, and they were roasting the meat on a sharpened stick, leaning close hungrily, one man testing it with a slash of his knife. Coffee brewed in a battered pot.

Drayton's first bullet sent it soaring into the air, splashing hot liquid into the face of one of the men. He reared back, clawing at his eyes, screaming. The second shot exploded the fire in a hundred directions and one of the others jumped about madly, slapping at flames on his greasy shirt front.

The third man shoulder-rolled backwards and when he came up facing Drayton's cover, he had a blazing six-gun in his hand. Drayton rolled to one side, worked lever and trigger and raked the fire area. The man with the six-gun went down, twitching as he lay on his face. The one with the burning shirt had reduced the flames to a smoulder in several places and his gun came up, firing wildly. Drayton put a shot into him just as the man with the scalded face snatched up a sawn-off shotgun and blasted a charge into the juniper bush. Drayton was to one side but several of the big double-0 buckshot took him in the left arm. He grunted, rolling, the arm flopping down to his side. The rustler bared his teeth and came running in, readying the second barrel. Drayton lifted to his knees and triggered the rifle one-handed. The shot punched dust from the rustler's vest and the man fired, but the tug at his vest threw his aim off.

Drayton dropped flat, got his six-gun out and working as the rustler ran up, roaring, raising the shotgun, aiming to dash the cowboy's brains all over the juniper bush. The man looked unstoppable . . .

Drayton's bullet knocked him back a couple of feet and the second shot hammered him to the ground where he lay groaning. Drayton kicked the shotgun out of reach, lifted the man's Colt from his holster and tossed it far into the brush. He tore off his neckerchief and wrapped it tightly about the three wounds in his arm as warm blood ran down to his wrist. He used his teeth to knot the cloth, watching the other two men all the time. Neither moved.

Drayton went out warily, holding the rifle with his blood-sticky left hand, cocked Colt in the other. There was no movement up at the shack, but it was deep in shadow and the cowboy moved warily as he disarmed the dead men, threw the guns towards the creek. He used a boot toe to turn them on to their backs but didn't know any of them. Then he turned towards the shack, moving out of line with the door and coming in from the side towards a shuttered window. But his precautions were unnecessary.

The shack was empty, stank of unwashed human habitation, and he lit the lamp on the table. It was a mess, a packrat running hurriedly out of the wash of weak light. There were spiders in the upper corners, too, and something that moved under one bunk that just might have been a snake. He guessed the cabin hadn't been lived in for a while, likely while the dead men outside had been out on rustling expeditions.

There was a potbelly stove and he got it going, heated water and bathed his arm which was swelling. He dug out two buckshot pellets but the third was deep and, he thought, lodged against bone. He knew it would give him trouble but he was unable to remove it, so re-bandaged the wound.

He hadn't eaten much during the long days of tracking down the rustlers and he went outside, salvaged some of the meat from the wreckage of the fire, dusted off the ash and dirt and sliced himself several steaks. He ate these slowly, drank from the creek and by then it was full dark.

Bringing down his horse, he ground-hitched it on some grass and spread his bedroll.

It was a restless night and he felt feverish from the wound. The arm was swollen badly come morning and he had to loosen the bandage. He ate some cold meat, drank creek water, smoked a cigarette and checked the cattle.

The count was exact: twenty-three prime beeves belonging to the Broken D spread where he had worked for the past three weeks as a top hand. Old Man Daniels would be pleased to get these back . . . but wait . . . he was closer to Amarillo here than the ranch. Seemed crazy to drive them all the way back to the ranch only to have to drive them into Amarillo later to sell.

Besides, he knew he would have to have a doctor cut out that buckshot. Back at the ranch they must think he — well, truth to tell, he didn't know *what* they'd be thinking about him. *A new man, disappearing without a word, twenty-some of the best cattle missing . . .*

Anyway, he decided, he would drive the cows into Amarillo. They ought to bring a good price right now. A *real* good price.

★ ★ ★

'He's a damn rustler, J.D.! I never liked the look of him right from the start . . . I told you so, you recollect!'

'Calm down, Ben, calm down,' J. D. Daniels said. 'Buck Drayton came with good references. I know the men he's worked for — '

'*Claimed* to've worked for!' cut in Ben Ivo, ramrod of the Broken D. 'Look, J.D., you an' me've been together a helluva long time now and I've always had the right to hire-or-fire — except in the case of Drayton. I just don't savvy it! And now look what's happened — the primest of our beef missin' for ten days and Drayton right along with 'em.'

7

Daniels, a man in his early sixties, worn down by the years, shook his head slowly. 'I know those references weren't forged, Ben. I *know* it. He could've been hurt in that storm. There've been wash-aways and landslides — how far did your men look?'

'Nigh up into the sierras. If he went in there, then he did it for only one thing: to hide them beeves.'

Old Man Daniels sighed, looking at the rugged foreman, a man only a little younger than himself, honest as the day was long, a fine cowman — but stubborn as an Idaho mule.

'Ben, we'll give him one more day and — '

'One more day and he'll have sold the cows and — '

The door of the cluttered ranch office opened and a cowpoke, sweaty and dusted, looked in and said somewhat breathlessly, ' 'Scuse me, J.D. — Ben, there's a rider comin'. Muff reckons it looks like Drayton!'

Ben Ivo heaved out of his chair,

staring at the cowhand. Then J. D. Daniels stood and reached for his walking cane: he had a reminder of Little Big Top at Gettysburg in his right leg which made it necessary for him to use the stick.

'Let's go see what he has to say, Ben.'

Ivo coloured a little, always a man who hated to lose, even a theory. 'He din' bring back any cows with him?' he snapped at the ranch hand and the man shook his head. Ivo gave Daniels a kind of smirking look and they all went out into the yard.

It was ten minutes before they were sure it was Drayton and another ten before he dismounted stiffly by the corrals and tossed the reins of the weary horse to the nearest ranch hand. His left arm was in a black sling but he took it out now and worked the fingers stiffly as he made his way across to where Daniels and Ivo stood waiting.

'Don't expect to find your job waitin' for you!' the foreman growled, but J.D. waved his cane, looking at Drayton.

9

The man was big, tall, wide, solid as a tree and mostly unsmiling. His face was battered and weathered from many years on the open range and he had the habit of moving his eyes without turning his head so that some of his looks seemed mighty hostile when they weren't meant to be. The eyes were brown and penetrating, and he swivelled them now from the foreman to Daniels.

The cane pointed to his arm, the white of a bandage showing under the sleeve. 'You didn't have that when you left, Buck.'

'Some buckshot. I dug out two but the one I left got infected. Held me up.'

'Doin' what?' Ivo asked tightly.

Drayton dug into his pocket and brought out a rawhide wallet, darkened a little in places with his sweat. He handed it to Daniels who leaned against the corral rails, cane hooked over one while he unfolded it. He took out a square of paper, read, snapped his eyes at Drayton, then took out some paper money. He smiled faintly as he turned to Ben Ivo.

'Seems Buck here located our missing steers and sold 'em to the agent in Amarillo. Here's the money.'

Ben Ivo's jaw dropped. He glared at Drayton. 'The hell told you to drive our beeves to Amarillo?'

'Was closer than coming back here after I found 'em.' He jerked his head towards the far distant sierras. 'Rustlers had 'em up there in a hidden canyon.'

They waited until Ivo asked impatiently, 'How many of 'em?'

'Three.'

'How many dead?' J.D. asked shrewdly.

'Three.'

'That how you caught the buckshot?'

Drayton nodded. 'Had to see a sawbones in Amarillo and he made me stay a day or two in the infirmary. Arm's gonna be OK . . . J.D., I'm about tuckered. Like to wash-up.'

Daniels nodded. 'Go ahead. Then come up to the house. I want more details, Buck. And I might have another job for you.'

Drayton frowned and Ivo stiffened but J.D. put away the wallet, took up his cane and began to limp back towards the house.

Ben Ivo spat and stomped away without a word.

★ ★ ★

J.D. Daniels eased back in his leather chair and looked across the parlour to where Drayton sat a mite uncomfortably on the edge of an over-stuffed chair.

'Many a man would've been tempted to take the money after selling the cows and just keep on riding, Buck.'

Drayton's eyes seemed hard as they settled on the rancher's face. 'I hire-on, I ride for the brand, J.D. Told you that when I first arrived.'

Daniels nodded. 'Yeah, I know — but it's true what I said: some would've kept the money and rid on out.' He held up a hand, staring levelly at Drayton. 'I can read men pretty good after all these years, Buck, and I knew right off I could trust you.'

'Ben wouldn't agree.'

Daniels smiled. 'Ben's over-protective. Thinks I can't take care of myself now I'm getting along in years . . . I can trust you, Buck. You've proved that by bringing back this money . . . ' The rancher's voice faded a little and there was a silence. Drayton rolled a cigarette, his left fingers still a mite stiff, and lit up as Daniels continued.

The rancher indicated the mantel-piece where several framed tintypes and photographs rested. 'Mrs Daniels died last year, we only had the one child, Boyce. That's him in that silver frame with the fancy edging.'

'That's a Texas Brigade uniform.'

Daniels smiled. 'You ever see it during the war?'

'Coupla times — over the barrel of a rifle.'

'Yeah — that's one reason Ben Ivo

13

doesn't take to you, Buck.'

'Once a Yankee, always a Yankee, eh?'

'Well, never mind that. Boyce — *Boy* we used to call him — came through the war without any serious wounds.' He paused. 'On his body, anyway. Took a good while to settle down, but then he grew restless on the ranch, began to drift, got into a couple of scrapes, one a shooting. Then we got word he'd joined the cavalry, went West and fought in the Indian wars.'

'Had me a little of that, too.'

J.D. merely nodded. His hands didn't want to stay still, fluttered here and there over his clothing, checking buttons, smoothing creases.

'Boy was badly wounded in some scrape up north — I have no details, just some sort of fracas with the Indians. Most of his troop were wiped out but somehow he managed to survive.' Another long pause. 'Then we had a letter from him — a farewell letter . . . '

Drayton, lifting his cigarette towards

his lips, stopped the motion, moving his eyes to the rancher, seeing the deep sadness gripping the old face.

'Boy was dying when he wrote the letter and he knew it. He said a man named Zac Landon was taking care of him and he asked that I give this Landon a job, or some kind of reward, because he'd spent most of what little money he'd had on Boy . . . '

Drayton frowned. 'Not many good Samaritans around these days, J.D.,' he said quietly.

'No — and I note your scepticism, Buck. I was leery, too, wondering if Boy had somehow been coerced into writing that letter. His handwriting was very bad, which we put down to his pain. Anyway, Landon never showed up. I wrote to him care of General Delivery, Cheyenne, never heard anything for a spell, then this . . . '

He took a piece of paper from a drawer, smoothed it out and handed it to Drayton. It had only a few words on it.

Sorry. He died. They were followed by a squiggle of pencilled lines that might have been *Z. Landon.*

Or it could have been anything, almost, the scribble was so bad.

'It came from Cheyenne,' Daniels continued, taking back the note and putting it away carefully in the drawer. 'I wrote the sheriff there but never got any reply. I wanted to know where Boy was buried, and I wanted to speak with this Landon — quite prepared to reward him for what he'd done for Boy. So I put a series of advertisements in several Wyoming and Montana newspapers, offering a reward for information leading to Landon and also asking Landon himself, if he read the ads, to get in touch.' He shook his head slowly. 'Seems he'd moved on and no one knew where. Buck, I just don't feel right about it. Here's a man who cared for Boy, was with him when he died and I haven't had a chance to even speak with him, let alone reward him.'

'You ever wonder *why*, J.D.?'

'Why a total stranger down on his luck would care for my son? Of course I did, still do — that's the part that haunts me, Buck. Like you say, good Samaritans are few and far between. Also, Mrs Daniels, on her deathbed — she just never seemed to find any reason to go on living once she knew Boy had gone — she made me promise I'd find Landon if I could . . . I've tried, but maybe not hard enough.'

'Just when did all this happen, J.D.?'

'Late last Fall, just before winter. Wrote to Cheyenne lawmen again and this time I got a reply, sayin' that Landon was a no-good drifter and gambler, had been in all kinds of scrapes, had even busted out of jail once. I naturally asked for more details but never got 'em.'

J.D. stood, foregoing the use of his cane, limped to a cupboard and poured them both drinks. He seemed to put his own down fast but Drayton only sipped slowly.

'I want you to find Landon for me,

Buck. And find Boy's grave and if possible bring me back his body so I can lay him to rest beside his mother. If Landon's still alive, bring him back, too.'

'Even if he's a no-good drifter?'

'I don't give a damn what he is. He took care of my son. That's all that counts with me.'

'J.D., you don't know much about me.'

'Know enough. You interested?'

Drayton was slow in answering. 'Don't like the cold: that's why I stay down south. It's spring here but it'll still be what you Texans call winter up around Cheyenne for another month or so. And *their* spring ain't any too warm . . . '

J.D. held the man's gaze. 'Is that a *yes* or a round-about way of saying *no*?' He leaned towards Drayton. 'Buck, I need this chore done — you in or not?'

2

North

Drayton was buckling the straps on his bulging saddle-bags when a shadow fell across him. He swivelled his eyes sideways, saw the scuffed, scarred old cavalry boots and knew it was Ben Ivo.

'Leavin' us, eh?'

Drayton went right on adjusting the saddle-bags, straightened and threw them across the back of the big smoke gelding. As he adjusted tie-thongs, the foreman edged closer.

'Listen, Yankee, you come back here, you bring back good news for J.D., savvy? *Good* news!'

Drayton turned, truly puzzled. 'What's that mean?'

'I gotta spell it out for you?'

'Yeah.'

Ivo curled a lip, scrubbed a hand

around his rugged jaw. 'Yeah — dumb Yankee, I oughta known. It's this way, Drayton, the war changed young Boy Daniels.'

'Changed a lot of men.'

Ivo looked at him sharply, having caught a trace of wistfulness in Drayton's words, but all he said was, 'It changed Boy for the worst. He come back all quiet and sour, managed to put on a smile for Grace — that was Mrs Daniels — but he'd turned mean. Was a good kid before he went, seen some pretty terrible things, I reckon, and he got into a few scrapes.

'Grace was bedridden, real sick a long time before she died. It wasn't too hard for J.D. an' the rest of us to keep Boy's troubles from her . . . '

'How big were these troubles?'

Ivo squinted. 'J.D. din' tell you then?'

'Said Boy had gotten a mite wild, was all.'

Ivo spat. 'A *mite*! Well, details don't much matter, but he near crippled a coupla fellers in a brawl, shot another

— din' kill him, but — well, it was one reason he quit this neck of the woods. Joined the cavalry under another name 'cause he thought he *had* killed that feller, I reckon.' He sighed, drilled his old, hostile gaze into Drayton. 'That's about all. We dunno nothin' about what happened up north . . . but whatever you find out, Boy'd reformed, gotten back to his old self, an' his last thoughts were of his parents . . . You got that?'

Drayton held the old man's gaze and slowly nodded. 'You and J.D. go back a long way, I guess.'

'Longer'n you can remember,' the foreman said curtly. 'You come back and tell him any different to what I said and I'll kill you, Yankee.'

Drayton turned back to his horse and swung easily into the saddle. He looked down at Ben Ivo and touched a hand to his hatbrim.

'*Adios*, Ben.'

★ ★ ★

He'd forgotten just how cold it got way north in these latitudes. Hell, this was their *spring*! He was glad he hadn't been here for the winter. But after he took the smoke gelding from the box car down at the rail depot, he rode into Cheyenne and first thing he bought was a fur-lined jacket. He put up with the smart remarks of the cracker-barrel set with their feet up on the warm potbelly stove, paid his bill for the jacket, a warm shirt and undershirt, some tobacco and coffee, and went back outside.

A bitter wind was sweeping in across the prairie and he found an alley where he changed his shirt and slipped into the jacket. *That* was better! Now he could get on with his chore.

It was around noon so he ate in a café he recalled from years ago when he had lived up in these parts. Different owners and lousy grub, but at least it was warm and it was cheap enough. He sat two cups of surprisingly good coffee on top of the leathery steak, smoked down a cigarette rolled from the fresh tobacco he had bought, and left a tip for the tired-looking waitress.

The sheriff had no time for him, told him he had been newly elected when the previous man had been gunned-down by a drunk six months ago. He said he'd never heard of Landon.

Drayton could tell he wasn't going to get anything more out of Sheriff Elton and left, booked into the Equality Hotel in a room already reserved for him at J. D. Daniels' request.

He left his gear there and washed up, went downstairs in search of the *Cheyenne Call*, the local newspaper. He was surprised to find the editor — *E. Bridges* — was a woman, and a quite attractive one at that. She was about thirty, was dressed neatly enough, although there was printer's ink under her fingers and a smear sweeping lightly across one cheek. She wiped her right hand on her apron before offering it to Drayton, smiling with good teeth and a deal of warmth, the skin around her eyes crinkling a little so that he figured in a few years she would have the beginnings of crow's feet. But they wouldn't detract from her strong beauty. As she gripped hands with him she pushed a strand of jet-black hair back from her forehead.

'Mr Daniels wired me you'd be coming, Mr Drayton. You've made good time.'

'Eager to get the chore done and back to some real warmth,' Drayton said, doffing his hat.

She laughed easily and opened the potbelly stove, threw on two billets of wood. 'That'll help — you Texans all seem to feel the cold.'

'Not a Texan. I was born in Nebraska, spent a lot of time around Cheyenne and Laramie and in the Dakotas. Then I woke up to the fact I didn't *have* to freeze my a — didn't have to freeze and went looking for a job down south.'

She laughed again, louder this time and he arched an eyebrow at her.

'Forgive me! But it strikes me as rather funny that you go all that way, find yourself a job, and before summer arrives, you get sent back up here!'

Drayton grinned ruefully. 'Always was lucky. J.D. says he'd been running an ad in your paper for a few months . . . '

She sobered now and nodded. 'Yes. Wanting information about a man named Zac Landon. Offering the reward might've seemed like a good idea but — well, it brought in all kinds of wild claims from all kinds of people. Mr Daniels asked me to open any replies and he trusts me enough to give an opinion about whether I thought they were genuine or not.'

'What's the percentage so far?' At her quizzical look, he said, 'The ratio of genuine to get-rich-the-easy-way hopefuls.'

'Oh — well, almost one hundred per cent have been fake claims. I haven't the resources to thoroughly check out each one, of course, but there's a certain tone to the non-genuine letters. Only two, I thought, might be genuine but while one did know a Landon it was the wrong one. The other had misread the name, thought it was London.'

Drayton held her gaze a moment and then nodded. 'You run this place yourself?'

'Yes. Well, I have a typesetter and printer, of course, but mostly I'm news-gatherer-cum-editor-cum-proof reader and sometimes distributor. My father started the paper, but he died a couple of years ago and I've been struggling on ever since.'

'You like it?'

Her smile lit up the room. 'Love it! Guess that makes me kind of crazy, but — well, Dad always said I'd been born with printer's ink for blood.'

'Always liked the smell of a print-shop.' Drayton indicated the silent hand press with the inked rollers and plate. 'But are there any replies to J.D.'s new adverts? He said he was going to run some and jump the reward to five hundred dollars.'

A small frown appeared between her eyes. 'I advised him against it. When it was only two hundred and fifty we had all those wild replies. Though I'm a little surprised this time that we've only had half a dozen so far . . . none of which seems genuine. But I keep a post box down at the general store and haven't been down for a couple of days. Perhaps you'd like to check there? I can give you a note authorizing you.'

'OK. Seems I interrupted you. Going to press soon?'

'Soon as you leave — oh, I didn't mean that as a dismissal. I just meant . . . '

He grinned. 'I understand, Miss Bridges. Thanks. I'll go see what I can pick up if you'll write me that authorization.'

★ ★ ★

The store was the same one where he had bought the warm clothes earlier and it seemed to him that the same loafers were still clustered around the potbelly when he made his way to the counter.

'Stopped shiverin' yet, Texan?' one man called, chuckling.

'Just about. Thought I might help things along with a couple of whiskies when I'm through here.'

'You need someone to steady your hand while you get 'em up to your mouth?'

Drayton waved it away with a grin and handed the surly looking counterman the note from Evelyn Bridges. The man stared at it for a long time.

'Like me to read it to you? Or I can tell you what it says,' Drayton said impatiently.

The man glared, walked over behind a sectioned-off part of the counter behind a wire grid, searched through a set of dusty wooden pigeonholes. He came back with three envelopes and dropped them on to the counter in front of the big cowboy. Drayton picked them up, flicked his hard gaze to the counterman.

'These've been opened. Two of 'em, anyway.'

The storeman shrugged. 'Not by me.'

'Who else then?'

'No idea. You want anythin' else? I'm pretty busy.'

'Friend, who opened these letters? You know it's an offence to tamper with US Mail?'

The man didn't seem fazed. 'You know, you don't listen good. I told you I'm busy. *Real* busy.'

'Yeah, I can see.'

The man walked to the far end of the counter nearest the stove and sat down, picked up a crumpled newspaper and began to read, lounging.

Some of the loafers laughed as Drayton stuffed the letters in his pocket, still glaring at the counterman. 'I might be back to see you.'

'Don't bother,' the man said without looking up. 'Next time I might not be so friendly.' He placed a six-gun on the counter, kept his hand covering it, still didn't look at Drayton. The big cowboy hesitated, then started for the street door. 'Name's Cody if you're fool enough to come a'lookin'.'

The loafers exchanged a few remarks with the storeman, but none of them took any notice of the man in the rust-coloured corduroy jacket who adjusted his hat on his head of red hair and slipped out the side door.

In his hotel room, Drayton rolled a smoke and lit up, sitting on the edge of the bed with the letters. He looked at them more closely. Yeah, two had been opened but the third seemed more intact.

In fact, the third letter seemed newer, less dirty or crumpled. Like it hadn't travelled far . . .

He opened the first two anyway and, as he suspected, it was clear someone was just trying to cash in on the reward. They were barely legible, which didn't mean a thing in itself, but the claim to know Landon was outlandish. One said he had 'gone to his reward in heaven' but the man's wife was able to make contact with the spirit world and so he was confident she could speak with Landon on Daniels' behalf. The other simply said: *I know Zack Langdon. The son of a bitch owes me money and if I can make some off him by ratting on him that's fine with me. See me at the bend of Cowbale Creek under the willows at midnight. Bring money, otherwise don't come.*

The third was neater, the paper cleaner, the hand firmer.

There was a man called Landon or somethin like it at Green River in Sweetwater County, six or seven month back. He was takin care of someone. Maybe I know where he is now. You wanta find out come to the

Drover's Nest saloon any night from eight on. I'll find you.

No signature. But there was something about the way it was written, as if a few words had been deliberately misspelled, last letters dropped: deliberately disguising . . . ?

He went to see Evelyn Bridges, but she didn't know the writing; thought, too, that it was probably worth following-up.

'Gives you an excuse to have a couple of beers, anyway,' she told him and he smiled faintly.

'Never need an excuse for that. OK. I'll go along early and see what I can find out.'

She became a little more serious. 'Just — be careful, Buck. Five hundred dollars is a lot of money, especially to some of the hardcases here in Cheyenne.'

'I know it. Let you know how it turns out.'

But the bar of the Drovers' Nest was crowded and noisy and he knew his correspondent had chosen the rendezvous well. Without even a name or a description he had no choice but to simply wait, hunched over a beer, eating a steak at a corner table, then going back to the bar for another beer to wash the leathery meal down.

Someone nudged him and he looked into the owlishly grinning face of a man in a rust-coloured corduroy jacket, his battered hat tilted back off his face to reveal sweaty red hair.

'Easy, friend. Spilled my drink, you did. Want to buy me another?'

'I'll give you a face full of fist for nothing. Give me some room there!' Drayton growled.

Red grinned wider, gave a little bow. 'Pardon me all to hell, cowboy, thought we might've gotten together, but . . . ' He shrugged and started to turn away.

33

Drayton grabbed his arm. 'What's that mean?'

'Means you ain't the man I'm lookin' for.' The redhead didn't slur his words now and was standing firm in the crush of noisy drinkers. Then he winked. 'Guess that wasn't fair comin' up on you like that. You read any good letters lately?'

'Maybe.'

'Ones that could be worth five hundred dollars?'

'Again, maybe. Hardly seems like the place to discuss such a thing.'

'Come over here.' And Red led the way to a corner behind the piano which appeared to be broken because no one was playing and the keys looked as if they had somehow been disrupted. He turned to meet Drayton, sober-faced now. He had pale eyes, freckled skin, and a wispy moustache which seemed to disappear every so often when the light washed over it. 'My name's Red McGee. Seen your ad, in the *Call*. Reckon I know this Landon. He's in town here, but he ain't usin' that name.'

'What name's he using?'

McGee grinned, held out a hand. 'Hundred in my palm and I'll tell you not only that but where to find him. If he's the one you want, I get the rest of the reward, OK?'

'I'll give you ten now.'

Red snorted, shaking his head, starting to move away. Drayton took him by the arm. 'Or I could push you out the side door here and beat the hell out of you.'

McGee was mighty sober now, alarm showing in his eyes. He was tall as Drayton, but more than fifty pounds lighter and he didn't look fit.

'Hey, take it easy! I'm tryin' to help you out here!'

'Trying to help yourself. You want ten dollars — or ten knuckles in the mouth?'

McGee swallowed, held up his hands, palms out. 'Well, they said you were hard. OK gimme the ten. Right. You know Cheyenne?' Drayton nodded.

'Down Applejack Street, third house from the end. Usin' the name of Miller. He don't go out much an' he'll be home now.'

'You come show me.'

'That weren't the deal! I don't want to go nowhere near that son of a bitch! He's mighty mean when he wants to be . . . '

But Drayton was pushing him out the side door into the night. Unfortunately, some drunken trail men were coming in at the same time and there was a lot of cussing and jostling and Red broke free, rammed an elbow into Drayton's ribs, and by the time Drayton had got his breath, the redhead had disappeared into the night.

Drayton swore softly, took out his six-gun from under his jacket and checked the loads before setting out to find Applejack Street.

And the man called Miller whose real name, according to McGee, was Zac Landon.

3

'Go Back to Texas!'

The house was easy enough to find and it was in total darkness.

Buck Drayton crouched by the rickety side fence, Colt in hand, nostrils damp from the cold bite in the air. He had been here for half an hour now and nothing had changed in the house. There were the distant sounds from the saloon area filtering through the crisp air but they weren't loud enough at this distance to cover any sounds that might have been made from inside the darkened house.

He stepped through a gap in the palings of the fence and reconnoitred the house twice, silently, and still there seemed nothing unusual about it. He listened under the windows but could hear no sounds of snoring from inside

— or any other sounds that might indicate life in there.

Making a decision, he went up on to the porch and tried the front door. Locked, of course. He made his way round to the back door and while it was on the latch he had no trouble forcing it. It made a noise and he went in crouching low, gun cocked in his hand.

Minutes later he knew the place was deserted and it had the smell of a house that had been closed up tight for some time. He took a chance, struck a vesta, found a lamp with oil in the reservoir and touched the flame to the wick.

The place had been lived in but not for some time, he reckoned. The clothes and over-stuffed parlour furniture smelled musty and there was a layer of dust on the mantelpiece. The ashes in the wood range in the small kitchen were stone cold.

'Red, you owe me ten bucks,' he said half aloud, set the lamp on the deal table and was leaning over to blow it out when a man stepped through the rear door into the kitchen, a gun in his hand.

Drayton blew out the lamp and dropped flat, hunkering beneath the table. The newcomer swore, fired a shot and Drayton heard the lead splinter the heavy table top.

'Come on out, Drayton! You can't get away — place is surrounded!'

From another room a man yelled, 'Judas priest, Pres! The hell're you doin'?' *Was that Red McGee's voice?*

Boots pounded down the short hall from the front of the house.

'Sonuver put out the lamp! He . . . '

The man grunted as Drayton rammed a shoulder into his midriff, wrapped an arm about thick hips and carried him back into the door jamb. The man's breath gusted out and his legs faltered. Drayton rose quickly and rammed a knee into an unseen face. The man groaned and fell away and Drayton leapt out into the yard.

He stumbled and was just straightening when a gun barrel or butt clipped him hard, knocking off his hat, driving him to all fours. Dazed, swaying, he started to get one leg under him when someone kicked it and he fell as the unseen gun bounced off his head again.

He had a vague notion of someone grabbing his shirt collar and dragging him back into the house. A door slammed.

When Drayton's senses cleared some, he was sitting on the kitchen floor, washed by the lamp light, menaced by three six-guns. One was in the hand of Red McGee but the man still looked nervous.

The man whom Drayton had tried to get past earlier was holding a kerchief over the lower half of his face. The cloth was soaked with blood from his nostrils. The third man was almost as big as Drayton himself and seemed to be in charge.

'Before you start anything,' this man said, as he opened his coat and turned so the light glinted on the deputy's star pinned to his shirt, 'look at this. Duly sworn lawman, feller . . . and you been caught red-handed.'

'At what?' Drayton asked, rubbing gently at the two knots on his head. His voice sounded strange to him and his ears were ringing.

'Breakin' and enterin', what else? Hell, lucky for you one of the neighbours seen you hangin' around . . . '

Drayton swivelled his gaze towards McGee. He curled a lip. 'You set me up, you son of a bitch!'

The deputy didn't even glance at Red McGee. 'You were caught here without lawful excuse. If you cain't convince us you had a right to be here, you're goin' to jail, feller.'

Drayton hitched to a more comfortable position and the three guns followed his every movement. 'Relax — I'm looking for a man named Landon. Got papers from J. D. Daniels, Broken D ranch, Deaf Smith County, Texas, to prove it.' He gestured towards McGee. 'That snake gypped me outta ten bucks and told me I'd find the man

I wanted staying here.'

The deputy smiled crookedly, looked at McGee. 'You up to your old tricks again, Red?'

The redhead looked a little sheepish and shrugged. 'I was thirsty and broke, Art . . . '

'You are a pain in the butt, Red, ol' hoss,' the deputy said. 'Pres, I think we oughta take this feller down to the law office, anyways. Sheriff Elton might like a word with him.'

'You're the boss, Art,' said the man through the bloody kerchief, and his eyes were bright now as he looked at Drayton, stepped forward and heaved the big man to his feet where he swayed a little.

Pres shoved Drayton towards the door. 'C'mon, you.'

'Red, you ain't gonna be in any trouble, but you'd best come along,' said the deputy.

'Aw, hell, Art, I have to?'

'You have to — now *move*, you goddamn rummy!'

They took him out the rear gate in the fence and down behind the buildings that lined Main. Drayton, still groggy, started to pull back against the grip Art and Pres had on his arms.

'Let's get up to where the lights are,' he slurred, struggling feebly.

'Oh?' Art said, sounding surprised. 'What you worried about, big feller? Figure somethin' bad might happen to you on the way to the jailhouse? Like — *this*!'

Drayton's legs were kicked from under him and he pulled Pres off-balance with a curse, but the man came with him, dropped on to him as he struck the ground, driving his knees into Drayton's belly. He lost his breath and pain burst behind his eyes.

A boot shook him as it slammed into his side. Another skidded off his head and lights swirled in a fireworks display. He was pulled half-upright and fists hammered at his face. Someone moved to get behind him — he thought it was Red McGee — and then there were

43

several savage blows hammering at his back and he wanted to throw up. His legs wouldn't support him and they let him drop and then the boots and fists rained down upon him, jerking grunts and involuntary groans from him, his breath hissing through loosened teeth. His mouth filled with the warm, salty taste of his own blood. Someone was standing on his right arm stretched out along the ground. He tried to use his left to swing a blind blow but he only struck a bony shin. Someone cursed and then there was a brief glimpse of a boot coming directly at his face and the night exploded, shattering into hundreds of brilliantly blazing shards.

He didn't remember the blackness engulfing him: just a distant voice saying, '*Go back to Texas!*'

★　★　★

Darkness. Smelly darkness. And noise. *Clatter-clank*, jerk and sway. More *clatter* screeches and strange forces upon his body that pressed him hard against some unmoving wall.

His head was thundering with noises on the *inside*, mixing with all the external sounds. He heard himself moan but didn't know why — until he tried to move in the impenetrable darkness. Then he groaned again — louder this time — as pain shot through his aching body, and all his limbs sent white-hot knives through his brain.

He was hurt. *Hurting*! And like *hell*!

He lay there, breathing in gasps that whistled through caked blood at the edges of his nostrils. One eye was stuck down so that he couldn't open it. Every tooth in his mouth ached and throbbed.

Drayton knew the feeling: he'd been in more than his share of knock-down-drag-out fights over the years — *Hold it!* His knuckles didn't hurt, didn't feel split or bruised, and they *always* did after a fight . . .

By God, he'd been hurt in an accident then! Or — or, he'd been beaten-up! Yeah, that was it. That explained all the throbbing agony in a hundred places and why his hands hadn't suffered from hitting bony jaws or hard heads. *He'd been given a working-over* — and it seemed he had been dumped afterwards.

He had no idea where he was. The noises and swaying continued and he still couldn't see a thing. It hurt, but he lifted one hand slowly and brought it up to his swollen face. He couldn't see anything although he knew that hand was touching the lashes of the eye that was operating. The hand moved to the closed eye and he managed to force the lids apart slightly, knew it was dried blood from a cut above the eyebrow that had caused them to stick. Not that it made any difference, he still couldn't see anything.

The smells grabbed his attention then. A mixture — gunnysacks? *Maybe.* Something dead? *Could be!* But it was vaguely familiar and he lay still concentrating, trying to recognize it. At the same time that he decided the smell came from bags of fertilizer, he recognized that he was on a train.

He was in one of the wagons with a tarp lashed over the top to protect the goods. Slowly, he groped above him and felt his fingernails drag across rough canvas. He had been dumped on top of the load, the tarp only inches above his head.

OK! It was stifling in here and he was sweating. It was hard, to breathe. He still wore his warm clothes and heavy jacket. Once he realized the air was foul, he began to gasp rapidly for breath, felt a panic uncoiling within his guts. It hurt like blazes but he managed to get up on to one elbow and his shoulder was pushing against the tarp then. One edge lifted slightly and icy air hit him in the face. He gasped again, but it felt good and helped bring his senses out of the mire where they seemed to be operating.

He held his face in the blasting stream of cold air, feeling his bruised flesh chill, and it helped ease some of the pain in his jaw and head. Thinking now, he groped in his trouser pocket, found his clasp knife still there. It was sheer agony opening the big blade and he figured at least one thumbnail was torn, but then the three-inch honed steel blade clicked out and he sliced open the canvas, sat up, working head and shoulders through the gap. It was really cold here and his teeth began to chatter. Stars shone above, but kept disappearing. At first he thought it was his eyes, but then he realized it was cloud wrack when he felt the spit of wet snow against his cheeks. There was a glow about the countryside beside the tracks and the way the long train was labouring he guessed it was climbing over a range. Balancing precariously on his knees, he looked around, saw the glow of the locomotive's firebox a long way ahead. The track was curving slightly. He looked back the other way, saw the freight car line ended two cars from where he was and then there were several box cars before the caboose.

A long night freight heading over the mountains.

And behind it, way behind, the drifting lights of a fair-sized town. *Cheyenne!* Had to be — for he was starting to remember now. The three men beating the living daylights out of him, a distant and distorted voice telling him to '*Go back to Texas!*' They must have dumped him in this freight wagon, lashed down the tarp and let the train ride him out of town. He put away the clasp knife and felt his creaking ribs, hoping none were broken. Anger began to stir in him. *The bastards thought they could scare him off! Just with a lousy beating! Oh yeah!* He rose to his knees, swaying and — whether he meant to or not, he was never sure — tumbled over the side.

His big body struck soft snow and he sank in a little, then began to slide. He threw out his arms, making his body T-shaped, slowing his motion. Panting, biting back against the jarring pain, he rolled over on to his belly and lay there, hands clawed deep in the snow bank and watched the train rattle on by. It was going very slow for the grade here was steep. It seemed to take an hour to roll on by. He watched the dwindling caboose, the almost invisible spark of the fire box disappear into the night, and, with all the noise suddenly no longer enveloping him, he felt mightily alone.

Now what, you crazy son of a bitch? he asked himself, speaking only in his head. Here you are, half dead from a beating, lying out on a high slope with snow falling, no hat, no gun . . . just what the hell do you think you are doing?

He knew, of course. At least his subconscious knew, long before he became aware of it.

He was going back to Cheyenne to find the bastards who had not only beat-up on him but had figured him for a man who could be scared off easily.

Buck Drayton didn't have much in

this world that he really valued. But he *did* have his honour and he valued that above all else — even his life.

It took him several tries to get on his feet and he held a hand over his eyes, straining to see through the gusts of light, spitting snow. Likely it wasn't snowing down on the prairie, just the chill of the high mountains causing this half-hearted fall. He saw enough to figure out where he was.

He had guessed pretty close, just using the way the train was climbing, the steepness of the track and the position of those distant lights. Now he had a reference and a direction.

All he had to do was start walking — and keep on doing so. If he fell into a snowdrift he would suffocate for there was no one to pull him out. If, in the darkness, he walked off the edge of the mountain . . .

To hell with 'if'.

He started walking, hugging his jacket close about him, longing for the warmth of a Texas riverbank in June.

Evelyn Bridges locked down the type forme and stepped back from the old printing press, using the back of a slim, ink-stained hand to push her hair up off her forehead. She pressed her hands into the small of her back, arching pleasurably, taking out the kinks.

The old cottage clock on the wall with the large Roman numerals told her it was 3.30 and she closed her eyes slowly. Another night with little prospect of sleep, but the old press had been giving a lot of trouble for a long time and last week she had lost a deal of revenue from advertisers because the ink had smeared on some pages, making the copy illegible, and hadn't even printed on others. Bill Merry, the printer, was too old now to expect him to work the long hours needed to repair the press or to contort his body into the various positions necessary to reach the offending nuts and bolts. He had been with her father when the paper had first opened and she was reluctant to ask him to retire, for she feared without the printing of the weekly paper to involve him, Bill would just fade away and die. The typesetter, young Lester Hallows, was too clumsy to turn loose on the ailing machine. So that left only herself . . .

I'll get a new one some day, she told herself, knowing how silly it was to cling to this monstrosity that was always breaking-down simply for sentimental reasons: her father had packed this press in piece by piece himself, unable to afford the freight, using mules and fighting blizzards. He had always claimed he had put so much of himself into this printing press that it was a wonder he was still able to function as a human being.

Now how could she destroy something with a history like that? She simply couldn't do it but she knew damn well that if she didn't get rid of it soon, the whole she-bang would go bankrupt — and then the paper that her father had devoted so much of his life to would be defunct. Still, if it didn't pay its way she would have to . . .

She was jarred out of her reverie by a rapid rapping on the streetfront window. Startled, Evelyn tightened her grip on the oily wrench she had been about to use to adjust the rollers, snapped her head around and gasped when she saw the face staring in at her.

It looked like some creature from the swamp: wild-eyed, hair standing on end, wet features contorted and swollen out of shape.

Then she recognized it for what it was: the face of an injured man.

As she approached the door, she made another discovery: the man slowly sliding down into a heap on her front sidewalk was none other than Buck Drayton, battered almost beyond recognition.

4

Big Gun

The girl came into the room where he had spent the last twenty-four hours and found him sitting on the edge of the bed. She came quickly around to him.

'What're you doing? It's too early for this kind of thing! Don't you realize you were suffering from exposure as well as the effects of that beating?'

Buck Drayton nodded, continuing to roll his cigarette, licking the paper edge, giving it a final twist and placing it between his lips. He struck a vesta and spoke around the cigarette as he fired-up.

'I'm OK now — I've taken worse beatings and once I was caught in a blizzard and had to have four toes taken off. You did a good job, Evelyn, putting me back together. I'm obliged.'

She leaned her shoulders against the wall, and he smiled slowly as he saw that faint smear of printer's ink just at her hairline. It was becoming almost a trade mark, he thought.

'I think I can read you, Buck Drayton. Your pride has been hurt as well as your body — you're going after the men who did this to you.'

'Uh-huh.'

She sighed and spread her hands. 'I always seem to be dealing with stubborn men — my father, Bill Merry, Lester the typesetter . . . '

'Stubborn's the best kind. We stick at a thing until we get it done.'

'Or get yourselves killed.'

'Well, I guess that's always on the cards — but you can get killed crossing the street. You ever noticed just how crowded and wild Main gets when another trail herd hits Cheyenne?'

'Don't try to change the subject. But really, Buck, do you feel well enough?'

He nodded, sober now. 'But I could

use a gun. My rifle's with my warbag in the hotel room and I've plenty of spare bullets but they kept my Colt.'

'I can lend you one — my father had several guns.'

'Fine. Now you're sure that Sheriff Elton's deputies ain't named Art or Pres?'

'I'm sure. I've been doing a little thinking and there was an Art Cregar and a Pres Solomon, a couple of hardcases, who appeared in town one time when there was some trouble with the trail men about paying some sort of tax imposed by the saloon. The leaders of the cowboys were found beaten badly and another was found floating in the river — it could be the same pair. Trouble-shooters.'

Drayton looked interested. 'Rough boys. Who hired them? The saloon man?'

'I expect so — Milton Gunn.'

'Powerful man?'

'Oh, yes. Has a big say in running this town, but it's rumoured he has interests in Laramie and all the way to Montana as well. He's a very dangerous man, has an eye on the fast buck, but no one's ever been able to prove the rumours about him. I think anyone who tried was intimidated or bought off and I've never been able to prove anything, either. I occasionally do an article on him, but he laughs it off, sends me flowers, for heaven's sake! He treats me as a joke; because I'm a woman, I suspect.'

'Doesn't sound so smart to me. How about Red McGee?'

'Oh, Red's a hanger-on. He'll do anything for a free drink. He's mean, too, and there's talk he's rolled more than one drunken cowboy for his trail pay. The other two could have hired him for a bottle of whiskey.'

'If he's a local, where does he usually hang out?'

She frowned, paused before replying. 'I know he sleeps in the livery loft sometimes and does chores there, or swamps out Gunn's saloon.'

'Could he have written that note?'

'If it was dictated, probably.'

'Two of the three replies I picked up at that store had been opened. The third hadn't, looked as if it hadn't travelled far.'

'Oh, I guess that's normal — Paddy Cody is a notorious stickybeak . . . but it's strange he didn't open all three.'

'I'd guess he either knew already what was in it or he'd been warned not to open it. Now, could you find that six-gun for me?' He glanced out the window at the early morning sky. 'You keep odd hours.'

'Penalty of running a newspaper.'

'Well, I'm glad I found you working when I got back from that train . . . '

She smiled. 'I'll get you the gun.'

Just like that. No attempt to talk him out of doing what he had in mind.

Drayton liked that.

★　★　★

He found Red McGee snoring off a drunk in the loft of the livery. The man almost screamed in terror when he was rudely awakened by a kick in the ribs and found Drayton towering over him.

He scrabbled away into a corner on all fours, eyes wide and staring, disbelief crumbling his face. He lifted protective arms across his eyes as Drayton took a step forward, grabbed the front of the man's filthy under-shirt and hauled him to his feet so roughly and powerfully that he almost slammed Red's head through the shingles of the sloping livery roof.

Red moaned, clapped both hands to his head. '*Judas*! Man, I'm dyin' — leave me alone. *Please*!'

Drayton smashed him back against the wall, pinned him there with one hand grasping the man by the throat. 'I'm gonna keep squeezing while you answer my questions, Red. Longer it takes, harder I squeeze. Got it?'

Red nodded, already making gargling, unintelligible sounds, toes barely touching the ground.

'I want to know who told you to write that note about Landon — was it Gunn?'

The man's eyes looked as if they would pop clear out of his head. He struggled, tried to tear Drayton's big hand away. The cowboy squeezed a little harder and Red's face began to colour up. He choked, shook his head vigorously.

'Who? Cregar? Solomon?'

Again Red's eyes seemed to bulge from their sockets even wider: he was shocked at how much Drayton apparently knew. And, hell, they'd only paid him off with a bottle of rotgut and a double eagle — wasn't worth dying for or being beaten to a jelly by this hulking giant.

He nodded. And suddenly the pain eased some in his throat and he sank down flatfooted again, off his aching toes, rubbing his throat, doubling over as he coughed and hawked. Drayton watched him and the man looked up,

'Gospel! They paid me to hang around the store, see who collected the note.'

Drayton believed the terrified man, brought up a vicious knee into Red's face. The man straightened as if on a spring, slammed back violently against the wall. Drayton's six-gun barrel knocked him unconscious in the stinking straw.

He left the stables by the rear door and went out into the weak early sunshine. Evelyn Bridges had said Gunn's saloon was called Casino Cheyenne and was at the far end of what the locals called The Strip, a section of town that housed most of the gambling saloons and whorehouses.

He had no trouble finding the place: it was still roaring this early in the morning and likely hadn't shut down at all. Which meant Gunn had greased quite a few palms. And would explain why he owned the biggest gambling concession.

Finding the place might have been no bother, but getting to see Milton Gunn turned out to be harder.

But not that much harder . . . not for Buck Drayton.

★ ★ ★

As he started up the stairs to the floor above, a slim man with a Mexican, or Indian look, stepped out from behind a curtain. He had his thumbs hooked in an ornate gunbelt that held two holsters, the butts facing forward for a cross draw. The man smiled, teeth flashing whitely against his swarthy skin.

'No, cowboy. This stairs only for special guests. Plenty booze and ladies down here for you.'

'How d'you know I'm not 'special'?' Drayton asked mildly and the man laughed, insolently running his eyes up and down Drayton's weathered clothing and the second-hand hat he wore, one of Evelyn's father's.

'I don't think you are special, *amigo* . . . and it is me who make the decisions who go up.'

Drayton nodded. 'How about who goes down?'

The gunman frowned and Drayton stepped close, rammed a short, punishing blow into the narrow midriff and the man grunted sickly and started to fold up. Drayton supported him, eased him back behind the curtain, saw a small cubbyhole there with a chair and hat rack, shoved the man roughly. He slid down into a heap on the floor, still paralysed by the punch to the solar plexus.

Drayton adjusted his hat, pulled the curtain right across on its slide, and went up the stairs two at a time. Another gunman was sitting against the wall, chair tilted back. He seemed surprised when Drayton's head appeared over the landing and was just getting to his feet when the cowboy came towards him, smiling.

'The Mex asked me to give you this.'

He brought his left hand out of his coat pocket and as the guard looked at it automatically, he took his Colt out from under the jacket flap and whacked the man across the skull. He eased him back into his chair, tilted the hat over the slack face and went to the first door.

It opened into the casino which was crowded although the noise was subdued and the room was half-obliterated in a fug of tobacco smoke. He saw most of the popular gambling games, a couple of private rooms opening off one wall. A hefty-looking man, far too large for the coat and pinstripe trousers he wore, started towards him but Drayton grinned, made a 'my mistake' gesture and backed out.

Two doors down he found Gunn's name on a door and went in quickly. An armed guard jumped up from a stool in a small vestibule and Drayton slammed the gun from the man's hand with his own Colt and rammed the barrel up under the man's ear.

'Friend, all I want to do is talk with Gunn — no hassle. Just take me in and you'll still be walking around with your head on your shoulders.' He propelled the man towards the inner door and a few seconds later was facing Milton Gunn across the man's carpeted office.

Gunn was an average-sized man, lounging in a chair behind his desk, reading a sheaf of papers through half-moon glasses that rested halfway down his thin nose. He flicked his gaze to Drayton and then to the guard who still had the gun boring into his neck under his ear.

'You're fired, Peebles,' Gunn said easily, folded the papers and put them on the desk, removing his glasses as he set his gaze on Drayton. 'I said *fired*, Peebles! Now get out.' As the guard started out, throwing Drayton a look of hatred, the gambler looked at the big cowboy. 'And who the hell're you?'

'Buck Drayton.'

Gunn stared back blankly. 'That s'posed to mean something to me?'

'You've heard of me. Man like you knows everything that goes on in a town the size of Cheyenne — you know why I'm here.'

Gunn frowned. He was a fit-looking man, sun-tanned, firm-skinned, sporting a dapper moustache and the suggestion of a goatee, but his hair was almost bleached and it was hard to make out the facial decorations. His eyes could have floated down with the first thaw, chips of ice, cold and expressionless. He half-smiled now and spread his big hands.

'Drayton — you'd be the Texan, sent by old J. D. Daniels, a man of some substance I hear.'

'Came up from Texas, but I'm not a Texan. You know J.D.?'

'Know of him. Had any luck finding this feller you're after?'

'No — the men you sent after me saw to that.'

Gunn frowned. 'What men would those be?'

'Art Cregar and Pres Solomon — and

67

you used Red McGee to sucker me in with a reply to the advert in the *Call*.'

Gunn was shaking his head even before Drayton finished speaking. 'Wrong, friend — way wrong. I've no interest in you or your business. Red sometimes swamps out the saloon for me. But he's a rummy and can't be trusted to tell you his own name. The other two, Art and Pres, well, I've had occasion to use their — talents — but if they gave you that shiner and the other cuts and bruises, it wasn't on any orders of mine.'

Drayton held the man's gaze and Gunn did not look away. Instead the man heaved to his feet and crossed to an ornate oak sideboy and lifted a decanter that caught the light coming through the window in such a blinding blaze that Drayton knew it had to be genuine crystal. Gunn handed him a drink.

'Guess you deserve a drink. You look like you could use one, but any man who gets past my guards . . . well, *salud!*'

He raised his glass and sipped. Drayton hesitated, then tossed down his drink, feeling its mellowness on his aching throat.

'Hell, man, it's meant to be appreciated! This isn't shotglass rotgut!'

'No. It tasted fine — but getting back to Cregar and Solomon — '

'Tell me what happened,' Gunn said, walking back behind his desk and Drayton almost smiled at the ease with which the gambler had turned things around, so that now Drayton was having to do all the explaining. But he didn't mind and told Gunn quickly and briefly about his mission and what had happened since his arrival.

'Guess someone doesn't want you to find this Landon.'

'Seems that way — you don't know him?'

'Zac Landon?' Gunn pursed his lips, took another sip of his whiskey and shook his head. 'Can't say I've heard of him, which doesn't mean he isn't in Cheyenne or hasn't been here. The other one — this Boy Daniels — never heard of him, either.' He gave the cowboy a warm smile. 'Nice meeting you, Drayton, but I can't help you. Like your moves, though. If ever you want to make a few extra bucks, look me up . . . I'll find something for you.'

'No, thanks — not right now.' Drayton seemed uncertain. He couldn't make up his mind whether Gunn was acting or telling the truth. The man was a pretty cool customer, unruffled. Look at the way he'd casually fired his guard when Drayton had dragged the man in at gunpoint. Another man would have raged, leapt out of his chair, thumped the desk, called for help . . .

He *seemed* open enough, but those eyes told Drayton that Milt Gunn was a ruthless man who would turn any situation around to suit himself, no matter what it cost.

'You want a hand of cards or to throw the dice in the casino before you go?' Gunn asked. 'I'll stake you one game.'

Drayton shook his head. 'Not right now. But I might be back.'

'Oh, well, now that's another thing entirely . . . you've been pretty lucky so far, but I wouldn't push it. Next time, I doubt you'd even get past the batwings.' Gunn stood, offered his right hand. 'Sorry we can't do business.'

Drayton made no move to shake the gambler's hand, kept his dark eyes on the man's fast-sobering face.

'If I need to see you again, Gunn, I'll do it. Thanks for the drink . . . ' He flicked his gun at the saloon man. 'Now be a gentleman and see me to the door.'

Gunn glared. 'You really *do* push it, don't you?'

'You coming?'

Milton Gunn came around his desk, face very stiff, those ice-cold eyes full of murder and hate. 'No one does this to me, Drayton!' he hissed, as he made for the door.

'Except me. Move along, Gunn.

Anyone tries to stop us . . . '

'Yeah, yeah! I know, you son of a bitch!'

Gunn wrenched the door open and there were two men with guns waiting in the vestibule, but he waved them aside and snarled for them to go ahead and make sure the way was clear to the batwings.

It was, although several hardcases stood by, awaiting instructions from Gunn. As Drayton stepped outside, the saloon man said, 'I like a man with gall, Drayton. That job offer still stands — and I will help you find this Landon. *Adios* — for now.'

Drayton said nothing, walked away quickly but no one attempted to stop him.

Upstairs again, Milt Gunn sat back in his chair and reached up for a satin cord and tugged it. A man appeared in a small doorway at the rear of the office within seconds.

Gunn was reading his papers again, didn't look up.

'Tell Art and Pres to get up here — and to come by the back way. I don't want anyone seeing them near this place.'

The man nodded jerkily and closed the door quietly behind him.

Milt Gunn set down the papers, pursed his lips and stared off into space.

Pity about Drayton . . . he really could have used a man like him . . .

5

Pursuit

'I wonder why they only beat you up and ran you out of town?' Evelyn Bridges mused as she served some lunch to Drayton. 'They could've killed you . . . '

Drayton swallowed a mouthful of food before answering. 'I think Gunn answered that: when he mentioned Daniels he said he'd heard J.D. was a man of some substance down in Texas. They likely wouldn't want to kill me and then find out they'd murdered someone who worked for a friend of the Governor of Texas or something. Gunn's too careful.'

She sat down with a plate of food for herself, cut a boiled potato in two and smeared it with a little butter and pepper and salt. 'I wonder how Gunn found out that J. D. Daniels is a man of 'some substance'?'

He glanced at her quickly. 'That's something I never even thought about . . .'

'Well, you feel you're at a dead-end now?'

He drank some coffee. 'I dunno, Evelyn. I feel uneasy about Gunn. He's pretty damn convincing, was quite open about knowing Cregar and Solomon and having used them at one time or another . . . but I still can't decide if he was genuine or not.'

'So what will you do next?'

He shrugged and they ate in silence for a few minutes. 'You said Gunn has interests all over the territory and into Montana — what kind of 'interests'?'

'Oh, saloons, gambling houses, whorehouses. He's part-owner of a stageline, has shares in some of those big Montana Cattle Associations. He's got his fingers in many pies. I believe he even lends money for people to buy land or existing ranches — and that when he forecloses he does so like an avalanche.'

Drayton nodded. Now he was getting a clearer picture of Milton Gunn. The man was a go-getter, had an eye on the fast buck — and the power that went with it. Likely owned half of Montana just by foreclosing on folk he'd loaned money to when they couldn't meet their repayments. Gambling and setting-up whorehouses were only marginally legal and were on the verge of coming under a blanket Federal law, so he could be looking to get out of such things and make himself legitimate.

Even if he had to do it by illegal means . . .

Drayton had seen such men before. And some had 'reformed' and really did stay legitimate, like Joe McCoy, the man who built Abilene, Kansas. But Gunn struck him as a man who would bend whatever law he had to so as to get to whatever destination he had set his heart on . . .

He looked at the girl across the table.

'Red McGee said Cregar and Solomon hung out mostly around Green River over in Sweetwater County. I believed him at the time, but maybe I'll go see him again before I take that trail . . . '

Evelyn was sober now. 'Buck, this is becoming a bigger story than I first thought. I saw good human-interest coverage in it but now — well, Milton Gunn is no one to cross swords with. Don't take chances where he's concerned.'

His gaze was steady, unflinching. 'Evelyn, I still have my job to do for J.D. He never said it would be easy.'

She smiled slowly. 'Funny, but that's just about the kind of answer I expected from you.'

★ ★ ★

Red McGee wasn't so easy to find this time.

The liveryman said he hadn't seen him since mid-morning, about the usual time he started to hang around the saloons, or went through the stack of empty whiskey bottles behind the saloons from the night before.

'He was pretty hung-over,' the man added.

Drayton searched the town, decided it wasn't worth spending a lot of time on, collected his rifle and warbag from the Equality Hotel and rode out.

From the upstairs window of Milt Gunn's office, the gambler watched him go, Art Cregar and Pres Solomon crowding in for their own look.

'Headin' west,' Cregar said. 'Likely goin' to Laramie.'

'Or clear to Green River if Red did what I told him to,' said Gunn, turning to look at the two hardcases. 'You think we ought to let Drayton ride all that way for nothing, gents?'

Big Art Cregar, quicker on the uptake than Pres Solomon, smiled slowly.

'Pres,' he said quietly, 'Go saddle the broncs — we've got us some ridin' to do.'

It was a long, cold ride west towards Green River and Drayton was beginning to wish he had stayed overnight in Cheyenne and set out in the morning.

But he figured he would make for Laramie and spend the night there in some warmth and comfort at a hotel. After all, J.D. was paying and he knew how Drayton hated the cold.

Then, during the afternoon, sleet came thrashing down out of the north without warning and it was so hard and was, obviously, hurting his mount so much, that he pulled over into a clump of trees, by a creek called the Wadcutter for shelter.

It was dark before the storm had blown itself out and by that time he had a fire going and had managed to brew some coffee and heat some beans with chopped-up jerky mixed through. It was a reasonably nourishing meal and he had no intention of trying to make a night run to Laramie. He ought to have started out much earlier so he built a rock-and-log wall beside his fire, threw on some heavy, slow-burning deadfalls and laid out his bedroll where it would get the greatest reflected heat from the crude baffle.

He tended to the horse, making sure it was comfortable and had shelter. Then he climbed into his bedroll.

It was sure warm — and took a heap of willpower for him to slip out of the blankets on the dark side and ease away into some nearby boulders, one saddle blanket wrapped tightly around his shoulders over his buttoned jacket, woollen shirt and long-sleeved under-shirt. He wore soft-leather gloves so there would be no chance of his flesh sticking to the cold metal.

Man, he needed his head read, taking on this chore!

But, although he had shaken the posse easily enough, he wasn't eager to chance that no one else was following.

He couldn't get to sleep. He was too cold and uncomfortable and had about made up his mind to creep back into his bedroll and into its warmth when he froze his own movement as he tried to settle more comfortably.

A night bird called.

In this cold? Yeah, that happened about as often as the cow jumped over the moon!

He thumbed back the rifle's hammer, a cartridge already in the breech, muffling the click of the ratchet with his gloves, ears cocked.

Another bird answered. That was left and right. Now — would the third call come from in front or behind . . . ?

It came from behind him and he wormed deeper into the crevice between the boulders, hearing them start to close in now that they were all in position.

He jumped when boots scraped on the boulder right above him and then the night exploded as three guns poured bullets into his bedroll, his hat flying and bouncing.

'Shoulda done what you was told,

Drayton!' said a deep voice on the rock above him, and Drayton rolled on to his back.

'I decide when I move on, Solomon!' Drayton said, as he squeezed the trigger.

Pres Solomon grunted and staggered, yelled as he lost balance and crashed down into the crevice only feet from Drayton. The big cowboy was lying prone by that time, shooting where he had seen the stabs of gunflashes when they had riddled his bedroll.

A man howled and then began sobbing: 'Oh, God! Oh, God! I'm gutshot!'

The last man was off and running and Drayton rolled out from under the boulders, somersaulting to his feet, working the rifle's lever. He glimpsed the man leaping from rock to rock, dropped to one knee, took careful aim and fired.

The man was in mid-air when the slug hit him, twisting his body, tumbling him in a heap at the foot of some rocks. Drayton leapt up and ran forward. The man must have been only wounded for his gun blazed and Drayton weaved aside as lead fanned his cheek. He stumbled and fell, losing his grip on the Winchester. Cursing as he rolled over, he snatched at his six-gun but had to lift the flap of the heavy jacket and by that time the killer had disappeared into the night.

He made his way back to the other two. The one who had been yelling about being gutshot was near death and Drayton let the man be.

At first he thought he had never seen him before and was just turning away when he looked again. Harder. It was Peebles, the man Gunn had fired for letting Drayton into his office. Well, he'd never need another job now.

Pres Solomon had only been winged by the rifle bullet as it ripped upwards across his hip and chest, mutilating his clothes, but only giving him a flesh wound. He had struck his head on the rocks as he had fallen and was only just now coming around.

By the time he had regained full consciousness, Drayton had him propped against a rock within the circle of firelight, wearing Drayton's jacket and hat, hands and feet bound.

Solomon looked at the big cowboy crouched, shivering, in the shadow of the boulders.

'Art comes back, he might put a bullet into you before he realizes it ain't me,' Drayton told him.

'Wha — ? Judas priest!' The realization of his predicament brought Solomon back to full consciousness with a rush. He struggled futilely against his bonds, looked around wildly. 'Art! Art, don't shoot, man! It's me! Drayton's over — '

Buck Drayton hit him with the rifle barrel and changed position, still staying in the shadows.

'Blabbermouth — you want to shoot off your mouth, hear yourself speak and enjoy that voice of yours, why you just start telling me why you fellers jumped me and why you don't want me to find Zac Landon.'

'Go to hell!'

Drayton reached out with the rifle, placed the muzzle against the other's right boot and fired.

The sound of the shot only partially drowned out Solomon's scream as the bullet shattered his big toe.

The man convulsed wildly, sobbing.

'That'll keep you outa the army if ever there's another war,' Drayton told the snuffling, writhing man. 'That leaves nine to go, don't it? But I was never much good at 'rithmetic. Maybe I'll switch to your fingers. I can see them better.'

'You — *sonuver!*' gasped Solomon. 'I'm bleedin' to death here!'

'Nah! Not in this cold. It'll congeal quick but then it's gonna ache like hell. Still you won't have much time to feel it because by then I'll be working my way through your fingers, starting with the thumbs. You know the human hand ain't worth spit without a thumb? Read that somewhere . . . '

'You crazy bastard!' sobbed Pres Solomon, voice not so deep and rich now, more a falsetto as the pain began in his foot and the hot muzzle of Drayton's rifle pressed against the base of his right thumb. '*Christ!* What d'you want to know? Gimme a break!'

'Just tell me about Zac Landon . . . '

Solomon moaned. 'I can't . . . they'll kill me! If Art's still out there he'll put a slug between my eyes . . . '

'Might be doing you a favour if you've got no thumbs to pick things up with.'

'No! Don't! Lemme get my breath . . . '

'Sure — You got two seconds . . . one . . . two — '

'*I dunno nothin! I'm just a hired hand!*' bleated Solomon frantically, cringing and at the same time bracing himself for the bullet that would remove his thumb — maybe not too cleanly, either. But it *would* be removed.

Drayton eased his finger on the trigger. Solomon was so scared he had emptied his bladder and the stench of warm urine made Drayton ease back. Solomon was breathing heavily, shoulders shaking.

'Gunn send you after me?'

'*Gunn?*' echoed Solomon, his voice shaking. 'Hell, no! We don't work for Gunn! Art and me're kinda — freelance, you know?' There was a lot of fear in Solomon's voice.

Then suddenly the man was throwing-up and when he had finished he began to scream curses at Drayton, ashamed he had let his fear get the better of him. He was nearly hysterical.

Drayton snapped at him to shut up, rose to one knee, head cocked in a listening attitude. Solomon hawked and spat, but one bleak look from Drayton kept him silent.

Drayton figured it was about time for Art Cregar to show up, unless the man had been wounded badly enough to incapacitate him somewhere in the boulders. But he couldn't hear anything. The night now was silent after the gunfire, the creatures of the creekbank not making a sound, sensing danger.

Solomon started cussing again and Drayton, fed up and a little on edge, reversed his hold on the rifle and clubbed the man into silence.

He thought he heard a sound out there, like a boot scraping across rock, but although he waited, poised for action, for twenty minutes, he didn't hear it again.

Solomon snored and Drayton swore softly, sweating a little despite the cold.

It was going to be a long night's vigil and it looked like the only one going to get any rest was Pres Solomon. And, of course, the man called Peebles who had died a little while back.

6

Laramie Lament

Solomon's toe was giving him pure unadulterated hell come morning. In fact, when he had come round during the night he had been unable to get back to sleep for the pain.

His moans and groans had disturbed Drayton who, although keeping watch, tended to doze every so often. He looked at the mangled toe, wrapped it in fresh bandages and told Solomon if he didn't shut up he'd put him to sleep again with the butt of the Winchester.

Solomon grunted and moaned despite himself but Drayton didn't club him: fact was, he even felt a little sorry for the poor stupid son of a bitch. It was obvious Solomon was one of those who followed orders but couldn't think much for himself. *Do this job,*

Pres — Do that — Move that stuff over there — There! There! you dumb mule!

Yeah, he could imagine the man's life being like that. But maybe he could work that to his advantage and get him to talk . . . *Later! In the morning . . .*

But Solomon couldn't or wouldn't tell him much. Only that Art Cregar had told him they had more jobs to do and he would be paid a bonus. The first 'job' was to stop Drayton anywhere along the trail.

'The second?' Drayton asked but Solomon looked at him blankly and shook his head.

'Art never said. He don't gimme more'n one chore to do at a time . . . '

Drayton swore to himself but he didn't doubt Solomon was telling the truth.

Thing was now — *where the hell was Art Cregar?*

He buried Peebles before they set off from the camp.

He rode double with Solomon while the man directed him to where he and

90

Cregar and Peebles had left their horses. There were none there, but after a little scouting, Drayton found two in the brush, still saddled and with trailing reins. Solomon told him that the chestnut was his and the grulla had belonged to Peebles. Cregar's grey was gone.

Buck Drayton checked the loads in his guns as he looked around. He had no doubt that Art Cregar was riding the missing horse. Somewhere. They'd found some splashes of blood amongst the rocks and on a tree in the clearing where Solomon said he and the other bushwhackers had left their mounts.

So Cregar was hit — but was he hit badly enough to run for cover? Or would he still dog Drayton's trail . . . ?

The only way to find out was to keep on heading towards Laramie. The skies were leaden again and Solomon looked gaunt and in pain. Drayton roped his wrists to the saddlehorn but the man wasn't going anywhere, he figured: he was eager to see a doctor about his foot.

He rode in silence.

Drayton rolled a cigarette and stuck it between Pres Solomon's lips and lit it for him. Solomon nodded, squinting.

'Obliged — You're a hellion, Drayton. Why you do this for me?'

The big cowboy didn't bother answering, rode on slowly, rifle butt on one knee, gloved hand covering the action to keep it warm. There was a little sleet, just enough to make it uncomfortable, but not bad enough to hunt cover.

'I never heard of this Landon till a few weeks ago,' Solomon said suddenly and Drayton dropped back alongside. 'Art just told me we was to stop someone who was comin' from lookin' for him — you ask me, he don't exist.'

Now Solomon was no great thinker, so Drayton wanted to know why the man had come up with such a notion.

Solomon shrugged. 'I never heard no one mention him but Art and Red. Peebles only wanted a crack at you 'cause you cost him his job . . . I just got the notion there wasn't no such feller as Landon. It was all hogwash.'

'Then why would they try to stop me finding him, Pres?' *Unless it was to make him think there was a Landon . . .*

Solomon screwed up his face. 'Hell, I dunno — Thinkin' ain't the best thing I do. Just a notion I got . . . '

He couldn't get anything more out of the man and a little while later he knew he would never get anything at *all* out of Pres Solomon.

They were riding through a draw, the sleet having eased and almost stopped, when there was a shot, followed by another hard on its heels. Pres Solomon grunted and slammed sideways in the saddle. His hands being still tied to the horn, he hung there, legs dragging as the chestnut shied and gave a half-hearted jump, trying to shake loose the weight pulling it to one side.

A glance told Drayton Solomon was dead, shot through the head, and then lead was buzzing about his own head and he spurred the horse into the cover of some rocks. Powdersmoke hung above the far wall of the gulch, near the exit and Drayton raked the area with four fast shots. He quit saddle, crouched low, waiting for retaliatory fire.

None came.

Then as the ringing subsided in his ears, the gunfire drifting away from the draw now, he heard the beat of hoofs.

He flung himself into the saddle, spurred down the draw and out the far end. A rider was a couple of hundred yards ahead of him, making for the timber. It was Art Cregar, by his size, and Drayton wasted two bullets trying to hit the man.

Cregar made it into the timber and kept on going. The stand of trees was thin enough at the edges but quickly thickened. A bullet ripped bark from a tree near Drayton's face and another ricocheted and nicked the smoke's chest. The horse shied wildly and reared and Drayton slammed against a low branch, twenty pounds of snow dumped into his lap and over his head. He spluttered and fought free and had to chase the spooked horse.

By that time, he couldn't even hear Art Cregar's mount and he knew he had lost him.

Wearily, he checked out the timber, found some tracks but soon lost them weaving amongst the close-growing trees. He gave up and went back to where Pres Solomon was still hanging from the saddlehorn.

That morning, before leaving the camp at The Wadcutter, Drayton had exchanged jackets and hats with Solomon again, so that each wore their own.

Which made it pretty damn clear to him that Cregar had *meant* to kill his sidekick and hadn't mistaken him for Drayton.

* * *

It was afternoon when Drayton rode into Laramie and it was raining. A cold

95

rain that soaked the sheepskin collar of his jacket and trickled down his back, freezing his spine.

He led the chestnut with Solomon's body roped across the saddle down Main and dismounted outside the small law office. The sheriff's name was Overholser and he was a grizzled man with rheumy eyes and a tobacco-stained frontier moustache. His clothes were old and worn, polished with age, frayed at the edges, specially his vest. In fact, the sheriff's star had dragged an outside pocket half-off the vest front, ragged stitches poking out like clipped wires.

He listened to Drayton's story about the ambush, said nothing, went outside and examined Solomon. His eyes were bleak as he returned, limping, rubbing at his left hip. But his right hand rested on his six-gun butt.

'What happened to his foot?'

'Toe got shot off.'

'From close-up, I'd say — Shoe leather's all burned from gun powder.'

'Yeah, he was cleaning his gun when it happened.'

Overholser made it clear that he didn't believe Drayton but didn't push it. He seemed only eager to get the formalities out of the way and, sighing wearily, brought out the necessary statement forms, a bottle of ink and two worn pens.

It was done quickly and the sheriff eased back in his chair, reaching around to massage his lower back.

'Goddamn rheumatics! — you're a blamed nuisance, Drayton, bringin' in that stiff. I just got through buryin' another feller with County funds, now this'n's gotta be done the same way. Council's gonna tear a strip off me a mile wide.'

'Didn't exactly plan it this way, sheriff,' Drayton told him and saw the wrinkled face straighten out. *Oh-oh! No sense of humour!* — He quickly changed the subject. 'Who was the other feller? Town deadbeat . . . ?'

Overholser scowled. 'He was a

deadbeat, all right. Scavengin' the whiskey bottle piles behind the saloons. Picked up one that had Prussic acid in it an' drank it . . . '

Drayton frowned. 'The hell was a saloon doing with that poison mixed in with its empty whiskey bottles?'

'Aw, they use it to prime baits for the rats — we got us a plague of the varmints right now. The Prussic's left over from the gold rush a few years back.'

'Gold rush? In Laramie? Hell, I lived up this way for years and I never heard of no gold rush in Laramie.'

The lawman sighed. 'Hell, you make a man downright tired, havin' to explain every goddamn thing! The rush weren't *here*! Was way back in the Medicine Bows. Short, but not so sweet . . . Claim-jumpin', murders . . . '

Drayton recalled it then, but he had been way over in the Dakotas and had never made it across in time to try his luck.

'Ended almost soon as it began and

some of the miners down on their luck sold off their gear for the fare home. There was lots of Prussic acid left over from refinin' the gold . . . just this redhead's bad luck he picked up the bottle . . . ' Overholser stopped in mid-sentence, seeing the look on Drayton's face. 'What's wrong?'

'The redhead who drank the Prussic — have a name?'

'Paper on him was addressed to a Wal McGee in Cheyenne . . . they say he was a rummy, used to do odd jobs in Cheyenne — know him?'

Drayton shook his head. 'No, not the man I was thinking of — what about Cregar, sheriff?'

'What about him?' snapped the lawman. 'If he shows up I'll pull him in for questionin'.'

'That's all?'

'All I can do. I only got your word he killed Solomon.' He looked up as Drayton stood abruptly. 'You're leavin' me to ask the Town Council for funds to bury this feller, huh?'

Drayton slapped some coins on the desk. 'That'll buy a headboard — I'll look for it next time I pass through.'

'Well, don't make that too damn soon,' Overholser growled. As Drayton left he began counting the coins . . .

The first man Drayton saw coming down the boardwalk through the light rain was Milton Gunn. He was flanked by his Mexican-Indian gunfighter-bodyguard.

The man looked confident in every movement he made, took it as his due when folk stepped out of his way.

Drayton stopped, holding his rifle, as Gunn and the Mexican came up, the latter's hot, black gaze on the big cowboy. Gunn seemed interested in Solomon's body.

'You do that to Pres?' he asked Drayton who shook his head.

'Art Cregar — Nailed him from ambush.'

Gunn snorted. 'Cregar and Pres were pards! Why would he bushwhack him?'

'No idea — You come for Red

McGee's funeral?'

Gunn looked at the big man carefully. 'Damn, but you're a nosey son of a bitch, ain't you!'

'Only way to learn things is to ask, my old man always said.'

'Sounds like good advice but it could get your nose tweaked, too.'

'Worse things've happened to my nose — *Are* you here for Red's funeral? They say the poor devil was poisoned.'

Gunn nodded slowly. 'Warned him he'd do something like that one day, scavenging amongst those empties tossed out by saloons — no, not here for any funeral, though I'll see the poor damn rummy gets a headboard or something. Every man deserves some kind of marker.'

'Here on other business then?'

Milt Gunn placed his hands on his hips, looking steadily up into Drayton's eyes. 'Drayton, I took a kind of a sneaky liking to you, the way you handled things back in Cheyenne . . . but you're rapidly startin' to piss me off. Now, stand aside and let me by, OK?'

Drayton moved aside silently and the Mexican curled a lip and managed to jar the cowboy with his shoulder as he passed. Drayton smiled faintly, unhitched his weary horse from the rail and made his way to the livery . . .

Halfway down the block, Gunn paused to light a cheroot he took from a crocodile-hide, silver-edged case, and turned his head as he bent over the match, held for him by the Mexican, so that he could see Drayton, just now turning into the livery stables.

'Raoul, send someone to go tell Sandy Reese to meet me in my office about sundown,' the gambler said quietly. 'And see it's done on the quiet.'

* * *

Drayton was tired, damn tired. *Must be getting old*, he told himself. *Never used to take me this long to recover from a fight or a beating* . . .

But the cold had eaten into his

bones, too, he rationalized. That was enough to make any man feel like curling up in a warm bed and not doing anything but sleep or dream.

Still, after stabling the smoke and seeing that the hostler was taking good care of the animal, he carried his warbag and rifle across the street to the Albany House and booked himself a room for the night. He arranged for a hot bath and afterwards, feeling much more alive now, went down into the town and had a few drinks, at the same time asking casually about Zac Landon.

At first, the men he bought drinks for were eager to please so they said, sure, cowboy, he was here not long ago . . . then between them, often contradicting each other's stories, they told him the kind of tales they figured he wanted to hear. But when the free booze stopped, so did the stories and Drayton moved on.

He asked here and there around town, at the stores, other livery stables, even in the stage depot, but all results were negative. It wasn't until he was leaving the stage depot that he noticed the name on the board above the yard gateway:

MEDICINE BOW STAGELINE
LARAMIE TO THE ROCKIES
CHEYENNE & POINTS SOUTH
Milton Gunn Prop.

Only then did he recall that Evelyn Bridges had told him that Gunn owned an interest in a stageline. Maybe that was what had brought the gambler to Laramie, some business connected with the line. Though it did seem a strange coincidence that Gunn and his Mexican should arrive just at the time that Red McGee was poisoned . . .

Could Red have been on the run, afraid of the way things were going in Cheyenne, and decided to make a break for it? Only to be caught up by Cregar and Solomon who then went back along the trail to wait for Drayton himself . . . ?

It was a theory that could be fact: he had a strong hunch that Gunn was in this much deeper than he admitted.

'Say, Texan! I was hoping to run into you again.'

Drayton gave a small jump at the sound of Milton Gunn's voice. He was outside a restaurant attached to the town's biggest hotel, The Valencia, and Gunn was standing on the steps near the entrance, talking with the Mexican.

Drayton walked across slowly, ignoring Raoul's snake-eyed look.

Milton Gunn watched narrowly and Drayton saw that he was being assessed — *For what?* he wondered.

'Getting to be more than a coincidence us running into each other, eh, Gunn?'

'Is *Señor* Gunn, mister!' hissed the Mexican but Gunn half-smiled and held up a hand.

'Take it easy, Raoul — you go find yourself something to eat and a little female company while Drayton and I talk over a meal . . .'

The Mexican stiffened. 'But, *Señor* Boss!'

'Relax, will you? Drayton's not going to do me any harm — that right, cowboy?'

'Wouldn't dare — not with a big bad bodyguard like the *señorita* standing by.'

Raoul was ready to draw but Gunn laughed, clapped him on the shoulder and sent him on his way. The gambler wasn't smiling when he faced Drayton.

'You want to watch it, friend — Raoul's got a mighty short fuse.'

'You seem able to control him.'

'But might come a time when I'm not around when he needs controlling — Anyway, I was just about to eat supper. Let me buy you a meal. You'll enjoy the food in here . . . '

Drayton didn't argue and was vaguely amused as Gunn put on a small show for him, snapping his fingers, having the staff running up instantly to see what he required. He glanced at Drayton several times, sidelong, looking for some reaction.

The cowboy figured he ought to make it good as part of his payment for the meal. 'Guess you've been here before. The staff all seem to know you.'

'Yeah — know I tip well. Believe in being generous, gets you good service . . . ' Halfway through the second course of broiled elk steaks and crisp roast potatoes with carrots and green beans and some sort of sauce, Gunn said, 'Felt a bit bad about this afternoon. Caught me on the hop — got some trouble with the stageline. Some sharp son of a bitch is milking me for a few dollars here and there and it's beginning to mount up — I've always made it a practice to pay my debts and owe no one. Like debts to me settled the same way. And the one thing I *won't* stand for is someone stealing from me.'

'Couldn't argue with you on that.'

Gunn's eyes narrowed. 'I hate the feeling that you're sort of laughing at me all the time, Drayton!'

The cowboy arched his eyebrows. 'Sorry if I gave you that impression.'

'Ye-ah — well, I was going through manifests and passenger lists and I came across a name might interest you; Landon — *Mrs Lauren Landon*. Passenger to Medicine Bow . . . '

Drayton set down his fork. He frowned. 'Hell, that's something I never thought about — that Landon might have a wife . . . '

'Well, I dunno if she's anything to do with the Landon you're looking for but it was a kind of coincidence — just thought I'd mention it.'

'How old was this passenger list?'

'Couple weeks, maybe three — Didn't go back much farther than that before I found where this smartass clerk was gypping me on the fares . . . details don't matter, but yeah, I'd say no more'n three weeks ago this woman rode one of my stages from Cheyenne, through Laramie, and on to Medicine Bow . . . we use a swing-station there. Not a very big place, so if that's where she got off you ought to be able to track her down quickly enough and find out if she knows this feller you're hunting.'

Drayton ate a little steak first before he nodded. 'Obliged, Gunn . . . I'll take a trip out there.'

'Stage leaves at eight in the morning —You can ride it at a concession rate if you want.'

'Thanks, but I'd rather take my own mount.'

'Suit yourself — but you could always tie it on behind, ride warm and snug . . . Only about fifty miles but weather's closing-in. Typical just before spring breaks up here. Like winter's having one last lash at us . . . anyway, you miss that stage there'll be others.'

'I'll sleep on it,' Drayton said, wondering why Milton Gunn was being so generous to him all of a sudden.

And why he *wanted* him to go to Medicine Bow so badly.

7

Delay

When he entered the cramped room that passed for the lobby of the Albany House Drayton thought he was seeing things.

There was a woman at the desk, her back to him, speaking with the clerk. He heard her book a room and then she rummaged in a tapestry purse for the money and he recognized Evelyn Bridges.

He stepped up beside her and before he could stop himself, blurted, 'What're you doing here?'

She looked up, smiling, handed the bored clerk some money and he spun the register towards her, gesturing to a pen and ink bottle while he made change. She wrote her name in the book.

'I'll give you three guesses,' she said to Drayton with a smile.

He felt a little foolish. 'Sorry, didn't mean to blurt out like that, but you're about the last person I expected to see when I came in.'

'You're staying here?' When he nodded, she added, 'I just arrived on the night stage. I'll be going back to Cheyenne tomorrow providing I can find a new part for my printer.'

He frowned. 'Laramie's a lot smaller than Cheyenne.'

'Oh, it's not a matter of finding some place that stocks the part. There's a retired engineer lives here, an old friend of my father's, and he's been making hard-to-get parts for my old machine for years. It's just about been rebuilt, I've had so many bits made for it.' She took a small shiny metal circle from her purse and two half-Moon bearings — obviously broken. 'If he can't repair these for me, I'm in real trouble this time. Might even have to close down. By the way, there's another letter arrived concerning Zac Landon. I opened it and I think you might have something this time.'

She handed him an envelope as the clerk gave her change, looked at the register, said to Drayton, 'You want your key?'

Drayton nodded, unfolded the paper inside, read quickly, lifting his gaze to the girl. 'This feller says he knew *both* Landon and Boy Daniels in the army! I didn't know Boy and Landon knew each other before Landon started taking care of him after he was hurt. In fact, Boy's letter gave the opposite impression — made it sound like Landon was a total stranger . . . '

Drayton took the key from the clerk who started fussing with the register and inkwell, wiping the pen nib and generally making himself busy. But his ear was hanging out a mile, although he did a good job of appearing totally disinterested in what the girl and Drayton were saying.

She stepped closer to Drayton,

pointed to the letter in his hand. 'See the address? Right here in Laramie . . . '

'Reuben Sadler . . . ' Drayton glanced up at the clerk who started to move away. 'You know where Cornmeal Street is?'

'Leads right down to Cornmeal Creek,' the clerk said a mite surlily. 'Turn into the street beyond Gunn's General Store and it runs off to the left. Not what you might call a good part of town.'

Drayton nodded and turned back to the girl. 'Kind of late to go calling tonight, I guess. I'll look him up in the morning.' He pushed a quarter across the desk.

The clerk smiled crookedly, pocketed the coin and moved away through a curtained doorway.

Drayton and the girl started up the stairs.

'I'd like to come with you in the morning, Buck.'

He slowed. 'Chasing more than a part for your printing press?'

She smiled, laid a finger alongside her nose. 'I smell a story. It was always going to have strong human interest but now — well, I recognize the signs of a newshound's hunch and my father said to never, but *never*, ignore it.'

'I'll buy you breakfast.'

Downstairs, beyond the curtained doorway, the clerk was waking the sleepy night guard in his little cubbyhole.

'Wake up, damnit, Foley! *Wake up!*' He shook the sleepy man, smelling the booze on his breath.

'Foley! Now listen, I have to go see Mr Gunn. Hear that? *Mr Gunn*! The man who owns this hotel? You watch the desk while I'm away. And if you don't do it properly, well, you know how Mr Gunn feels about his men makin' mistakes.'

That brought Foley fully awake and he scrubbed a hard-knuckled hand down his beefy face, squeezing the sleep from it. The clerk smirked and put on his hat as he hurried out the side door.

* * *

'The desk clerk was right,' Evelyn Bridges said as she and Buck Drayton turned into Cornmeal Street the next morning which was overcast. 'This isn't a very nice place.'

'Houses are tumbledown and neglected. Don't mean the folk are cut-throats, or drunks, or lechers — just poor.'

Evelyn looked faintly amused. 'You're a strange one, Buck Drayton — You have a very liberal outlook. At times.'

He grunted and pointed to a picket fence with several panels leaning drunkenly into a neglected yard. A frame house of unpainted timber, weathered a scabby silver-grey, stood behind it, a few wooden toys among the weeds.

At the door, Drayton eased open his jacket a little making sure his six-gun was ready should he need it. In answer to his knock, a woman with untidy hair and a young child astride her hip stared up at him. She was a Negress and her eyes were big and round.

'Yes?'

'Mrs Sadler?' The eyes grew rounder, but she didn't reply. 'This is Miss Bridges, from Cheyenne, and I'm Buck Drayton from Texas. Your husband wrote me a letter.'

He held up the letter Evelyn had given him last night. The woman barely glanced at it.

'Must be some mistake. I don' have no husband. He run out three years back.' She tried to close the door, but Drayton got a foot between it and the frame.

'*Reuben* Sadler, ma'am? Was he your husband?'

The woman shook her head and the baby began to squirm and protest, trying to get free of her mother's grip. 'Like I said, there some mistake — that no-good husband of mine was named Nate. Now you go away. I got five kids to look after.'

Evelyn pushed to the fore. 'Mrs

Sadler, there could be some money in this for you.'

The woman hesitated, seemed unsure, then swiftly shook her head and started to push against the door again. 'You go 'way, hear? You — go!'

Drayton easily resisted her pushing, shoved the door open roughly so that the woman stumbled and he went inside, bringing up his six-gun. He glimpsed some children and one of them screamed and started to cry and he also saw a lean black man hunkered down by a chair — and big Art Cregar holding a young girl about fourteen, his gun down at his side.

But when he saw Drayton he brought the gun up fast and fired at the same time that Drayton shot and all the children clapped hands over their ears and began to cry and the black man dived for the floor.

And Art Cregar swore as his gun spun away and slammed against the wall and the young girl turned and clawed his face with both hands.

117

Drayton pushed her aside, holstering his smoking six-gun as he reached for Cregar. The man slapped the girl hard, knocking her sprawling halfway across the room and the black man on the floor wrapped his thin arms about Art Cregar's lower legs.

Drayton stepped in and swung a punch into Cregar's mid-section and the man grunted, doubling over. Drayton hit him alongside the jaw and he kicked free of the Negro's grip, stomped on the man's head, and swung a backhanded blow at Drayton.

It took Drayton across the side of the head and he staggered and Cregar made for the door. Drayton got upright and launched himself in a headlong dive as Big Art went through the doorway. Drayton's rush carried them both across the narrow porch and out into the weeds of the yard. They grunted as they hit the ground and were wrenched apart by the impact. They rolled away from each other, bounced to their feet, and, crouching, ran together, teeth bared in their mutual hatred.

The big bodies hit and shook with the shock. Heavy fists worked and flailed like hammers, grunts of effort and involuntary sobs of pain mingling. Drayton parried a left hook in front of his face, ducked his head under Cregar's arm and slammed an uppercut home. Cregar staggered and gave Drayton room to swing a more telling blow. It nearly tore Big Art's head off his shoulders and he floundered backwards, arms flinging wide. His legs buckled and he went down to one knee. Drayton reached him with one long, driving step and put a knee into the middle of the man's face. Cregar went down, rolling, suddenly spun around and kicked Drayton's legs. The big cowboy staggered and Cregar came up with a rush, driving the top of his head at Drayton's face.

If it had landed it would have shattered the cowboy's jaw and crushed his nose back level with his cheeks. But

Drayton wrenched his head aside and Cregar fell to hands and knees with his effort. Drayton kicked him in the ribs and the man groaned loudly, collapsed and tried to roll away and climb to his feet all at the same time. Drayton stepped forward, kicked him again, the blow lifting the man several feet across the weeds.

There was cheering from the old house porch.

Cregar was crawling away now, one arm hugging his ribs. His hat had fallen off and Drayton twisted his fingers in the man's unkempt dark hair, yanked him half upright and hammered his other fist into the agony-twisted face.

This time Cregar stayed down, barely conscious, rolling about, hugging himself, face a mask of blood. He ended up on his side with knees drawn up and lay there, glazed eyes staring at nothing, choking on pain.

The young girl ran down and began kicking wildly at him with her large bare feet, sobbing. Drayton hauled her away and she turned on him, reaching for his eyes, but stopped when she saw who it was.

'That — trash! He done rape me!' she sobbed and Drayton handed her over to Evelyn who hurried forward to comfort the girl.

Drayton motioned to two boys, obviously twins, about eight or nine. He pointed to the woodpile. 'You boys grab yourself a billet each and if that man tries to get to his feet — why, you do whatever you have to. You savvy?'

Two brilliant white grins answered him as he went into the house where the woman was tending to the thin black man who was coughing rackingly into a stained piece of floursack.

'He been poorly since the soldiers threw him out,' the woman said, touching her own narrow chest. 'All that dust in the lungs from years and years of ridin' for his country and they — they don' even give him a pension!'

'Bureaucrats are mighty hard sometimes, ma'am,' Drayton said quietly, pulling a straightback chair across to sit facing Reuben Sadler, waiting for the man to stop coughing.

The woman went with her baby into another room where Evelyn Bridges had taken the young.

'That true about Cregar raping your daughter, Reuben?' Drayton asked grimly.

The man nodded. 'He say we send you away or he do the same to my wife and send my chil'en down to Mexico. He say I gonna be mighty sorry I wrote that letter to you.'

'Forget him for now. Tell me about Boy Daniels and Zac Landon.'

Reuben smothered another cough, spoke with the cloth covering his mouth. 'There money in this?'

'Depends.'

The black man nodded. 'Don't usually mess in white folks' stuff, but we a poor family, as you see. I been readin' 'bout that Texas man gonna pay five hundred dollars for stuff 'bout his son. Well, I decided to write that letter, 'cause we sure can use the money.'

'Don't worry about the money right now, Reuben. You were in the cavalry with both Boy Daniels and Landon? I mean, you all soldiered together?'

Reuben made a strange sound and it took Drayton a few minutes to realize the man was laughing. 'Not *together*, suh! Not in the *cavalry*! But I know what you means. I was a trooper and Boy was in command of our troop. Just a sergeant he was . . . Zac Landon, he was some kinda clerk but him an' Boy kinda buddied up, used to go on furlough together, hooraw the towns an' so on. Always in scrapes — and then Landon got hisself into trouble over sellin' off some army gear — a few guns, but other stuff, too, like canteens and boots an' blankets. They figured he needed help to smuggle the things out and said Boy was the one helpin' him, usin' the troop's wagons and so on.'

This surprised Drayton but he remained impassive. 'Was it true?'

The thin shoulders shrugged. 'Dunno

. . . but it don't have to be in the army when they's on the warpath agin their own men. They wants a — a — '

'Scapegoat?'

'That the word. Yeah, suh, a *scapegoat*, cause they likes to get army scandal cleared up fast. They court-martial both Boy an' Landon and they s'posed to go to jail, but they broke out before they moved to the labour camp They — they was popular, more reckless than mean, but that Boy, he could turn mean at times. Had bad headaches. Anyway, they got away and then the Injun Wars started up somethin' fierce and I guess the army just never bothered . . . I dunno. Then they say my coughin' gave away the troop's position up at Wagon Box Canyon and we lost a lot of men and they discharged me. *Unfit*, they said, but I was fit enough to carry a rifle an' sabre and fight them Injuns all them years . . . '

Drayton nodded, sympathetic to the man: he had run up against military callousness before.

'You wrote to me hoping to get the reward, Reuben,' Buck Drayton said slowly, bringing the man out of a brief, bitter reverie. 'What happened with Art Cregar?'

After Sadler had finished coughing, he said, breathing heavily and wheezing, 'He come round late last night, busted in, grabbed Hattie — that's my oldest girl — and said she stayin' with him all night and anyone try to leave or make a fuss, he snap her neck — and we better not let you in when you come in the mornin'.'

'How'd he know I was coming?' Drayton asked, but almost immediately remembered the clerk fussing around while he and Evelyn were discussing the letter. Hell, he'd even asked the man for directions! 'It's OK, Reuben, I know now. What did he say was to happen after I went away?'

'Say we can get on with our lives an' if ever we write any more letters to white folks, they come an' burn my house down — with my family in it.'

'Who's *they*?'

Reuben looked away, shaking his head.

'Come on, Reuben! You got an idea.'

'Mister, I in enough trouble. You gonna ride out, but me an' my family still gotta stay here . . . '

Drayton swore softly, but nodded curtly. 'Yeah, all right. But I reckon it could be Gunn behind this.'

He watched the black man's face, saw, the eyes widen and the fear boil in them at mention of Gunn . . .

Then there was wild yelling from the yard and Reuben tried to get up.

'My — boys!'

Drayton lunged for the front door, leapt across the porch, saw the twin boys sprawled on the ground and Big Art Cregar disappearing into the timber down by Cornmeal Creek. Even as he started to run forward there came the clatter of hoofs and he knew he would never catch the man.

He turned to the boys who were

sitting up, one crying, the other rubbing violently at his head.

'C'mon into the house, fellers. You done good, real good. And I'm gonna see you both get some strap cherry candy, OK?'

The crying stopped and the tears miraculously dried up.

It turned out that Reuben Sadler didn't know where Boy Daniels or Zac Landon might be and he was surprised to hear that Boy had died. But he did have some information that, while perhaps it didn't qualify for J.D.'s reward, was certainly worth something.

And it was unsettling, too.

Zac Landon had worked in the paymaster's office and part of his job was to arrange the various routes for the monthly pay trains to the many forts in the northwest.

No one seemed to remember this and the routes Landon had worked out for months ahead were still adhered to.

Until one day, a few months ago, when a large force of masked men attacked a particularly rich pay train during a blizzard. There was a wild gun battle and both sides lost men. The raiders were forced to scatter as army reinforcements arrived — a cavalry troop travelling behind the pay train that had heard all the shooting.

The outlaws were never caught and the payroll was never recovered.

* * *

In Drayton's room, while Evelyn tended to the cuts and bruises on his face and knuckles, she said, 'I recall that raid — it was particularly brutal and at first they thought it must have been Indians until the blizzard stopped and they dug some bodies out of the snow and found out the raiders were white men dressed up as Indians. It was hinted that some inside information had been leaked because the route was supposed to be secret.'

'And maybe Zac Landon was the one — after all, he set the routes long before he was court-martialled,' Drayton finished. 'Yeah, possible. He somehow got help and they pulled the raid, but the blizzard, and that cavalry troop, turned everything on its head . . . '

'We've been hearing about the bad shape Boy was in, but no one seemed to know how he had been injured — perhaps it was during the payroll robbery.'

'Yeah, that's about what I figure, too. Leaves quite a bit unexplained, but it's starting to make some sort of sense.'

She stood back and looked at his face, dabbed with yellow patches of iodine and arnica. She smiled. 'You look like a piebald Chinaman!'

He laughed briefly.

'Will Reuben get some kind of reward from Daniels, do you think?'

He looked at her sharply. 'I'll see he's rewarded.'

8

Medicine Bow

The stage journey to Medicine Bow was a boring one for Drayton and he slept most of the way.

He had gone to Sheriff Overholser and told him about Art Cregar's treatment of the Sadlers.

'Aw, son, now why you dump this in my lap? Sadlers is only Nigras. We don't have the money or time to spend on their troubles. 'Sides, they prefer to handle their own hassles in their own way.'

He jerked back in his desk chair as Drayton came around the desk and towered above him. 'Now see here . . . Overholser, the Sadlers are *people* and Cregar done 'em wrong. Hell, you ought to be after the son of a bitch anyway for bushwhacking Pres

Solomon. Now you've got the rape of a fourteen-year-old girl to charge him with — *fourteen year old*!' Drayton reached down for the stained vest and hauled the startled lawman clear out of the chair and brought his wrinkled face up to eye level. 'Now I've got you off your ass, don't you sit down again until you bring in Art Cregar! Savvy?'

He let the sheriff fall back. The old man *harrumphed* and straightened his vest, making a pathetic attempt at being outraged. 'You're headin' for trouble, Drayton! I'm warnin' you . . . '

'Aw, shut up, Overholser, before I hit you. Now you get after Cregar, and I'll take care of the Sadlers.'

The sheriff frowned. 'What you mean?'

'I'm sending 'em to Texas. Been burning the telegraph wires all morning and J.D. Daniels has agreed to take 'em into his ranch, find work for Reuben and his wife.'

'Aah, Reuben ain't gonna live long!

He's got the lung disease.'

'Texas is warmer and drier than up here. He's got a better chance down there and J.D.'s gonna give it to him.'

Overholser seemed mildly surprised then said, 'Seems to me, you're the one givin' 'em the chance.'

Drayton ignored that. 'Happens to be an army troop heading south out of the fort, so the Sadlers are travelling with them and they'll pick up a train along the way. Now you do your part and find Cregar.'

'Er, you wouldn't take a temporary deputy's badge, I s'pose?' The look on Drayton's face was answer enough. 'No din' think so . . .'

Drayton left the man buckling on his gun-rig and went in search of Milton Gunn. No luck. It seemed the man had left town.

When the stage pulled into Medicine Bow, Drayton unhitched the weary smoke gelding from the boot and went into the swing station for a wash-up and a meal.

Over the food — which was surprisingly good and plentiful — he asked if anyone knew where Mrs Landon lived.

The wife of the station agent said she *thought* that was the name of a woman who lived out near the edge of town.

'Keeps to herself,' she added casually. *Too* casually, thought Drayton, puzzled a little by the way she spoke, as if she was reciting something she'd been told to say. The woman saw him studying her and gave a quick on-off smile. 'Been a few rumours goin' the rounds, but you expect that when a pretty woman lives alone away from other folk — you know what I mean.'

Drayton could guess, but didn't reply other than to thank her for the information and ask for directions how to find Mrs Landon's house.

He saddled the gelding and rode on out.

The small frame house was in much better condition than Reuben Sadler's, the yard tolerably weed free, some narrow flower gardens along the edges of the path and a small vegetable plot at one side. The gate hinges weren't oiled and gave a banshee screech as he opened the gate and started up the path to the house.

The front door opened before he reached the porch steps and a woman stood framed there, one hand holding the door, the other down at her side, lost in the folds of a gingham house dress that had seen better days but was clean.

She was small and curvy, with maybe a mite too much lip rouge and eye make-up. He figured she was pushing thirty away as hard as possible and liked her upswept hair. And despite the plain dress she had a mildly disturbing effect on Drayton and she knew it. She would affect most men that way, he figured. She automatically touched her hair and smiled.

'You're early, cowboy, but come on in. Want some breakfast first?'

'Just eaten thanks . . . you Mrs Landon?'

'Of course.' She stood aside for him to enter and he saw that the hand that had been lost in the folds of the skirt held a small pistol. She laughed briefly at his startled look. 'Just a precaution — I live alone, you see.'

'No man to protect you?' Drayton said, going into the small parlour which surprised him some. The furniture was nothing to write home about but the cushions blazed in garish colours: bright reds and yellows and greens and blacks. It reminded him of some whorehouses he had seen.

She put the gun on a small table beside an overstuffed chair and sat down. Still smiling warmly, hands clasped now. 'Do I come recommended, or did you just ferret me out from local gossip?'

He sighed. 'Ma'am . . .'

'Oh, call me Laurie. It's more friendly.'

'We get much more friendly at the rate we're going and I don't think I could stand it.'

She laughed. 'You don't look the shy type!'

'Mrs — Laurie . . . just let me tell you a story. Not a long one. Just — just wait a minute and let me tell you why I'm here, all right?'

She looked kind of wary and curious at the same time, nodded, and he briefly told her about J.D. Daniels. By the time he had finished, the welcoming smile had gone and she looked much more sober now, a small frown between her eyes.

'What is it you want from me?' she asked quietly.

Not what you were expecting, Drayton told himself, and aloud, said, 'I want to find your husband. If his name is Zac.'

She nodded. 'That's him — I can take you to him but . . . ' She paused.

'He won't like it?' Drayton prompted, having picked up the notion along the way that maybe Zac Landon was a lot more complex than anyone had given him credit for.

'Is it worth anything?' she asked, avoiding his question.

'Well, I guess if you wanted you could be in line for the reward that J.D.'s offering. He'll pay for 'information leading to the whereabouts of Zac Landon' . . . that's what he says so — yeah, there could be as much as five hundred bucks in it for you.'

She brightened. 'Now that's better! I'll just put on a warm coat . . . '

While she fetched it he looked around the strange parlour again. There were tintypes scattered about the mantelpiece and a couple of small shelves. Laurie Landon was in most, wearing various costumes as if she were playing a part on stage . . . sometimes alone, sometimes with other people, men and women, also costumed. But there was no wedding photo, nothing he could pin down as being Zac Landon, and he realized he didn't even have a description of the man.

Then she returned with a heavy woollen coat and scarf and hat. She flicked her gaze at him briefly, smiling, striking a slight pose, one hand raised above her head, the other arm flung wide. 'I see you've discovered my dark past. Once I was a — shudder! an *actress*!' She whispered this as if it was a word that shouldn't be spoken aloud.

Drayton smiled, but seemed a little preoccupied as she led him outside, saying, 'Zac's not very far . . . '

Before they reached their destination, climbing a small hill slightly west of the cottage, he knew where they were going. He paused and she went on a few steps before stopping and turning.

'Come on! It's not far now.'

'No — just to Boot Hill.'

Her face straightened as he gestured to the arched gateway at the top of the hill, some of the headstones just visible above the curve of the ground.

'You said you'd pay for information 'leading to Zac's — whereabouts' . . . you didn't say he had to be alive!'

Drayton took her elbow, urged her up the hill. 'Show me,' he said tautly and

she led him through the arched
entrance, wandered down between lines
of graves and stopped at one near the
southern boundary of the cemetery.

The pine headboard said simply:

Zachary Landon
Age 27 years
Sadly Missed
by his
Loving Wife Laurie

'When did it happen? And how?'

'A couple of months ago. He'd
apparently been robbed and beaten and
when he fell he . . . hit his head on a
rock.'

There was a catch in her voice and
she turned quickly and hurried away,
taking a small lace handkerchief from
her purse and dabbing at her eyes.
Drayton followed her in a few minutes
and when he reached the entrance saw
she was already nearly at the foot of the
hill, hurrying back towards the cottage.

Drayton followed and when he

reached the house found her sitting in the parlour, now dry-eyed, hands clasped in her lap, waiting for him.

'You'll be wanting to know about Boy Daniels, of course,' she said and he nodded, sat down and rolled a cigarette, watching her closely.

He listened, but not with his full concentration, as she told him how she had helped nurse Boy Daniels with his horrific injuries — she didn't know how he came by them.

'He died in his sleep if that'll be some consolation to Mr Daniels.'

'Where's he buried?'

She blinked. 'Wha — ? Oh, Zac took care of that. I don't know where he took Boy's body . . . but he didn't bury him on Boot Hill.'

'Why not? It being so close and all.'

'Zac said we'd be in trouble for not reporting that Boy had been shot and tortured and . . . ' Her voice faded-off.

'You want more time to get your story straight?' Drayton asked abruptly, and she snapped her head up, stared, frowned, the small mouth tightening briefly. Then innocent puzzlement crossed her face.

'I don't believe I know what you mean, Mr Drayton.'

'C'mon, Laurie, or should I call you Sandy? Sandy Reese was the name you used on stage. Saw you once in Dodge City in some English musical thing with sailors and pirates ... when did you change your name?'

Her eyes were defiant now. 'When I married Zac Landon, of course. My real name *is Lauren* ... I don't think I like your attitude much, cowboy!'

He blew cigarette smoke towards her. 'You acted like a whore greeting a customer when I arrived ... pretty convincing, too.'

She gave him a sly smile. 'Then I haven't lost my touch, have I?' Her face straightened and she said, 'I — I had to *live* after Zac died! I want to return to acting, but well, I'm getting old by stage standards and the kind of roles I'd be offered wouldn't be to my liking.'

'Show me your marriage certificate, Sandy.'

'I will not! If you can't take the word of a lady then you can go to hell!'

He laughed. 'Haven't met many *ladies* who'd say *that*, Sandy! Look, did Gunn put you up to this?'

'Gunn? I don't believe I'm familiar with anyone called Gunn.'

'That'd surprise me. He seems the type who'd get *familiar* pretty quickly with a woman like you.'

She brightened. 'You think I still have my looks, then?'

'You're attractive enough — not a bad actress, either. But I don't want any more lies!' His voice had hardened as he said this and she jumped a little. 'Look, Milt Gunn bent over backwards to have me come here to see you — I believe he had a couple of hardcases named Solomon and Cregar try to kill me but when that didn't work out, he figured another way to throw me off the track of Zac Landon — send me to see his *widow*. He paying you much?'

142

She glared and curled a lip and called him a name no *lady* would even know let alone use. 'He said you were a smart son of a bitch! All right. I work for him in Laramie at present, though sometimes in other places.'

'In one of his whorehouses?'

'I ought to scratch your damn eyes out!' Her bosom was heaving now with her angry breathing. 'No! Not *in* one of his whorehouses, I *run* the biggest one for him! Or I will do when I tell him I've carried out this — chore — successfully.'

Her teeth tugged at her bottom lip.

'What happens if you're not successful? If you haven't convinced me that Landon's dead?'

'Oh, sweet Jesus, don't even think of that!' She leaned forward. 'Look, it's true! Zac Landon *is* dead, buried up there on Boot Hill. I don't know the full story, but somehow he ran foul of Gunn and although he didn't say so, I think he had Cregar and Solomon kill Zac. He wanted me to tell you the story about him dying after being robbed. He arranged things. This isn't a big town as you know. Almost everyone here depends on Gunn for a living — they'll do whatever he says. They fixed up this house for me and you ask anyone on the street and they'll tell you the Widow Landon has lived here for a year or more and her husband died after being rolled for what little money he had . . . '

Drayton believed her now. It fitted the picture much better. But left a lot of questions still unanswered.

Why would Gunn have Landon killed?

What really happened to Boy Daniels and where was he buried? And how did Gunn fit into the story? That payroll robbery . . . ? It could all fit — somehow . . .

'Will you — will you go back to Texas now?' she asked hesitantly.

'Hell, no . . . would you?'

'Yes! Yes, I would! I — I'd take things as they are and go back while I could. I know nothing about Cregar and

Solomon trying to kill you but Gunn for some reason has given you this chance and you're a blamed fool if you don't take it!'

There was a kind of plea in her voice and on her face. But he had to remember she *was* an actress.

'Can't do that. I'm not satisfied with what information I've got. I'll stick at the chore until I can tell J.D. what really happened to Boy and if possible take the kid's body back home.'

'Oh, you damn fool!' She leapt to her feet, eyes blazing now. 'Don't you see? You'll only get yourself killed! Oh, damn you — you'll get me in awful strife! Gunn made it pretty clear that it was up to me to convince you to quit looking now . . . '

'Maybe I would've — if you'd been able to show me Boy's grave.'

She made a helpless gesture. '*I know nothing about him*! Only what Gunn told me to tell you. Can't you see, I'm not *involved* in this! It's just a job Gunn wanted done and he picked me to do it.

Oh, come on, Drayton! All you have to do is tell this Daniels that his son's dead and so is the man who cared for him. That you weren't able to find out where Boy is buried . . . Look, if it'd make you feel better, I could . . . ' She edged down the top of her bodice and Drayton smiled, shaking his head. 'You lousy son of a bitch!'

He held up a hand. 'Don't feel insulted, Sandy — I find you attractive, all right, but you can't do anything to make me give up on this and go back to Texas. It's just the way I am. I take on a job, I keep doing it until I'm finished.'

She sat down, shaking visibly now, pale, drawn. 'But you'll ride away and I — I'll have some of Gunn's men come to see me and haul me up before him and when he finds out I didn't convince you, he'll — '

'Kill you?'

She laughed hollowly. 'He wouldn't be that forgiving! No, he has interests everywhere, even down in Mexico. He'd have that damn Raoul ship me all the way down there to one of their meat-houses . . . You know what they are?'

Drayton knew. Whorehouses south of the Rio where the girls were used up and then dumped, or ended up with their throats cut and left out for the coyotes.

He was beginning to work up a decent-sized hate for this Milton Gunn . . .

'You want to come with me?' Drayton asked.

She blinked. 'Wha-at? You'd protect me . . . ?'

'Do my best.'

'After what I was trying to do to you?'

'You were just trying to survive, Sandy — we all are. We have to do what we can. I can't *guarantee* to give you protection, but I'll give it a damn good try.'

She sat there, teeth tugging at her bottom lip. 'I — I'm scared, Drayton! Scared *not* to go with you and scared to say I will go!'

He stood abruptly. 'Well, you choose, Sandy.'

'Wait! Suppose I tell you something else, could you get me that reward money?'

Drayton was halfway to the door by now, halted and turned. 'It'd depend on what you had to tell me, Sandy.'

She had to force herself to do it, he could see that. She swallowed and he knew instinctively that her fear and reluctance were genuine enough.

'Suppose I tell you that Zac Landon's *not* dead at all? That he's hiding-out somewhere and I know where. I think it must be Boy Daniels in that grave I showed you. I don't know why or how, but — I'm telling the *truth*, Drayton!'

'How come you know this?'

She smiled crookedly. 'Men say some strange things when — you know. They like to try to impress in case they don't — perform as well as they'd like to. And, like you said, a girl has to do what she can to survive.'

Drayton came towards her and she started to back away. 'Sandy, don't play with me. If this is another of your acts . . . '

'No! I swear it's not! I do know where Zac Landon is! It's a place called Sierra High, an old gold mine up in the Medicine Bow Range. I've sent some of my girls there when Gunn told me to. I guess he wants to keep Zac happy. He ordered me up there twice . . . I'll take you to him — for the reward money.'

9

Last Chance

Buck Drayton left the nervous girl at the house while he went into town and hired a horse for her, doing a deal with the agent at the stage swing-station rather than the livery in the middle of town where he could be more easily seen.

Maybe it was a mistake: the agent had been bitching about Milton Gunn being a skinflint when the stage had arrived and while Drayton had been eating the meal served by the man's wife. He seemed to dislike Gunn intensely and his wife had actually snapped a warning at him twice, telling him it was foolish to talk like that in front of a stranger who had just ridden in on the stage at concession rate.

So Drayton had figured if he hired

his horse from the agent, there would be little chance of anyone reporting it to Gunn or his men.

He never did find out exactly what had happened, but when he returned to pick up Sandy Reese, walking into the parlour and calling out that they could get underway as soon as she liked — there were two men waiting. Men with guns. One was Art Cregar.

And Sandy was huddled on the sofa, white-faced, looking desperately afraid.

'Figurin', on takin' our top whore somewheres, Drayton?' asked big Art Cregar with a grin that must have hurt, the way his mouth was all battered and swollen.

The other man stayed close to the girl and Drayton made no hostile moves.

'I figured you were wounded along the trail, Cregar. We found blood where you picked up your mount, Pres Solomon and me.'

Cregar's smile vanished. 'You winged me, you son of a bitch, but my damn rifle jammed and it took me a long time to work my way back to where the hosses were. Then I got the idea of followin' you and Pres — he always was a dumb bastard an' I knew he'd break if you started to work on him . . . '

'You've had yourself a time, of it, haven't you? Bushwhacking me first, then your pard — and topping it off with the rape of a fourteen-year-old girl . . . '

Cregar curled one swollen lip. 'She was only a Nigra — not worth the effort. But, nev' mind that stuff — you an' the whore ain't goin' nowhere. Mr Gunn give you your chance and you blew it — and so did she.'

'So what happens now?'

'We-ell . . . it ain't unusual for whores to git beat up, even killed by their customers sometimes . . . '

Sandy gasped and put the back of a hand to her mouth, her eyes widening. Cregar winked at her. ' 'Course to make it look good, she should have her clothes all torn and be what's that big word they use? Violated! That's my part. Oakey, there, he's one of them queer types like to watch but not be part of it . . . '

'Shut up, Art!' snapped Oakey and Drayton was surprised to see the man flushing in embarrassment.

Sandy whimpered and pressed back into the sofa.

'And how do I end up? Arrested by Overholser?' Drayton asked.

Cregar laughed. 'That old daisy! Hell, no, he's too damn lazy. You gotta be found dead, Drayton. Sandy here, she always carries a ladies' gun . . . like this!'

Cregar brought out the small gun Sandy had held when Drayton had first arrived. It was nickel-plated, slick, and he almost dropped it, fumbled and grabbed at the weapon.

Drayton knew he would never have a better chance.

If Cregar had his way it would be his *last* chance at anything . . .

Luckily, he had come in with his coat

unbuttoned for no other reason than it was an instinctive precaution. Now, as Cregar fumbled for the nickel-plated ladies' special, Drayton swept the flap aside and palmed up his Colt even as Oakey spun towards him, shooting. Drayton was moving as he drew and hurled himself aside, triggering as his feet left the ground, three fast shots.

One missed and thudded into the wall but the other two hit Oakey and sent his rail-lean body hurtling backwards across the small room. The man's arms flailed wildly, then his narrow shoulders crashed through a window, glass tinkling, frame wood splintering, the sounds mingling with Sandy's muffled scream as she covered her face and dropped to her knees beside the sofa.

Cregar let the ladies' special fall and brought up his six-gun, blasting at Drayton's big figure. The cowboy struck the wall, bounced off and hit the floor rolling. He triggered and Cregar staggered, half-twisting as Drayton fired again. But the killer's turning body made him miss and then Cregar, holding his side and bent a little, emptied his gun.

Four bullets tore up the floor into splinters and whirling sections of ragged linoleum. Some struck Drayton in the face and he covered it with his hands, half-blinded. Then Cregar snatched a chair, hurled it through the window on his side and dived after it into the yard. Drayton's gun hammer fell on an empty chamber and he leaned down and scooped up the small calibre ladies' special, almost dropping it, then saw Cregar's legs disappearing below the window sill. He got to his feet and snapped at the shaking woman to stay put, and then charged out the front door.

This time Cregar wasn't getting away.

The man was staggering down towards the rear fence, still holding his side, and Drayton pounded after him, firing once and hearing the small crack of the gun. He rammed it into his pocket: it would take more than a .32 calibre rimfire to stop a man of Cregar's size.

Something like a man Drayton's size . . .

He increased his pace and Cregar stumbled and blundered his way over a sagging panel of fencing.

Then he saw the big cowboy coming, relentless, deadly. He snarled a curse, ripped a paling free of the cross-pieces and almost fell as he cleared the fence. Drayton vaulted the sagging part in one running leap and was within reach of the startled Cregar in seconds. The killer turned, swinging the paling with both hands.

Drayton ducked, feeling the wind and hearing the *swissssh!* as the length of timber just cleared his head. He ducked under the next swing, rammed his head into Cregar's chest and pounded two hard fists into the man's face. He staggered, stumbled, dropped the paling and lunged for the small creek that ran behind the house.

He was wading frantically for the far side when Drayton reached for him, twisted fingers in the man's hair and yanked back hard. Cregar came around swinging, pronged his fingers and tried to gouge Drayton's eyes. The cowboy knocked the hand aside, hit him in the throat. Cregar choked and gagged, floundering, chill water soaking both men now. He thrust a hand into his coat pocket and brought out his clasp knife, staying out of Drayton's reach as he used his teeth to open the blade.

Grinning balefully, more confident now that he had a weapon, he slashed air in front of Drayton, took a lunging step forward, making an upward strike. Drayton flung himself aside and the blade snagged his jacket flap, ripping it a little, the knife not coming free right away.

He swung a backhanded blow that took Cregar in the middle of the face. The man stumbled and fell to his knees, dragging the knife free at last and slashing wildly. Drayton grabbed the arm and snapped it at the elbow across one knee. Cregar screamed and fell back, sinking under the surface. Drayton placed a boot on the man's chest and pushed him to the bottom, placing his weight forward, pinning the man under the muddy water.

Cregar thrashed and kicked and bubbles burst through the surface as Drayton, his face as ugly as it would ever get, pressed down relentlessly, kneeling on the man now, feeling the struggles weakening, pressing — pressing — until finally the struggles ceased. He continued holding the now motionless Cregar under for another minute, and then eased back, grabbed the man's jacket and heaved him out on to the bank.

He wasn't a pretty sight, but he wouldn't be bushwhacking anyone else or raping fourteen-year-old girls anymore . . .

*   *   *

The girl was very quiet as they cleared town by the back streets. Not that the place was very large, but it seemed to have more than its share of stickybeaks, judging by the number of curtains that moved at windows as they rode past.

Once clear and heading across the creek *away* from the distant Medicine Bow Range — in an effort to confound the peekers — Sandy Reese said quietly, 'How could you stand to kill a man with your bare hands?'

He flicked his gaze towards her, characteristically not moving his head. 'Cregar wasn't no man. Wouldn't call him an *animal* because that'd be insulting them. It's not a nice feeling, Sandy, but drowning Cregar won't keep me awake nights.'

'No.' She raised a hand and lightly touched her bruised and swollen cheek. One side of her face was puffy and he had noticed the bruising on her forearms, too. Also she tended to wince once in a while when she took a deeper breath than usual. 'He was a cold-blooded killer. The rumours were that he had killed more than a dozen men for Gunn.'

'Liked to beat up women, too.' Drayton kept his sidelong gaze on her, saw her snap her head around towards him, alarm showing on her face. 'You didn't have that face or the arm bruises when I left to fetch you a mount, Sandy. You tell him much?'

She was silent, staring groundward, face flushing. When she looked up again, her eyes were moist. 'I — I don't like pain and he was threatening all kinds of — vile things. I'm sorry, Drayton. I had to tell him about you.'

He nodded. 'I savvy that, Sandy. Did you say where we were headed?'

Another silence. 'I — I truly don't know if he asked that — no! *Honestly* Drayton! You can't see all the things he did to me while Oakey held me . . . I was nearly out of my head. He may've asked and if he did I probably told him, but I *just don't know*! I know I'm a coward but I can't help it!'

'Easy. They're dead now. We'll keep riding this way until we're out of sight of town and then I know a way through some dry washes and old draws that'll bring us onto a trail into the hills. Once we hit the Bows, you'll have to lead the way to the mine.'

Her face had a strange look. 'You take things very coolly.'

She wasn't acting now: she was truly afraid . . .

'Best way to think things out. Look, Sandy, I should've thought about someone watching you . . . I should never have left you alone. Anything that happens now is not your fault. So don't feel bad about it, OK?'

He was surprised to see a tear roll down across her swollen cheek. 'Oh, Drayton, where the hell have you been all my life! You're not like any other man I've ever known.'

He smiled crookedly. 'I'm no different to anyone else. When I was trail driving we could've run into each other. Not with you on the stage, but in your other role.'

'Oh? You're saying you frequented whorehouses?' She sounded amused now.

'Not 'frequented', but I'm just saying I have the same needs as any other man.'

'But there's a difference — you act like a *real* man should. A *gentleman*.'

'Hey! You'll have me going all *gawsh an' swooney* in a minute! C'mon, if you can stand it, let's put the spurs to these mounts . . . '

★ ★ ★

About two hours later, he knew someone was following them. They had swung towards the Rockies and, in amongst some boulders at the base of a butte, he dismounted, climbed a tall rock and looked along the back trail.

He didn't see anyone, but there was a faint yellow mist hanging in the air about where they had crossed a small stream, and the haze was on *this* side of the stream. Likely whoever it was was looking for their tracks: he had covered them pretty well after they rode up out of the muddy water but he knew a good tracker would find sign to read and follow. The girl was waiting anxiously for him to climb down, grabbed his arm, looked intently into his face. He nodded.

'Someone back there — at the stream. They haven't found our direction yet but they will.'

'Oh, God! If Gunn catches me now . . .'

'He won't. We'll lose 'em in that tangle of dry washes yonder. They might have a notion we'll be heading for this Sierra High, but they won't find any actual tracks that'll clinch it for 'em.'

She shook her head. 'I was a damn fool! This isn't worth a lousy five hundred bucks! I should never have mentioned Sierra High.'

'But you did, and here we are, and if you want to get out of this with a whole

163

hide, Sandy, you're gonna have to keep your part of the bargain and do just like I say. I don't want to scare you, but from what I've seen of Gunn and the way he operates, I figure it'll be a whole lot worse for you than me if they catch up to us.'

'You son of a bitch!' she hissed. *'Don't want to scare you,* you say, and promptly proceed to do exactly that! You've got a mean streak in you, Drayton, you know that?'

'No, and the longer we stay here trading insults the better the chance Gunn's men've got of cutting our trail.'

'Damn you! There you go again! Making me sick to my stomach . . . '

But she followed him willingly enough and he led her on a twisting, dizzying trail through the old watercourse and in the end she admitted she didn't have any idea where they were.

'About a mile from where we started out to throw 'em off the trail,' he told her and saw her jaw drop.

'But we must've travelled at least ten miles!'

'A bit more. But by the time Gunn's men do the same, we'll be climbing the high trail into the Rockies.'

She moaned and wearily set off after him as he spurred away.

* * *

From high up the slopes of the Medicine Bow Range which was really part of the foothills of the Rockies themselves, they saw the dust trails of the pursuers, twisting and turning through the maze of dry washes and draws, way, way back.

Drayton grinned. 'They'll never get out of there before dark. We got far to go?'

'We'll have to camp out tonight . . . I don't think I could find the place in the dark.'

Drayton nodded but cursed inwardly — a night camp at this height in the awesome Rockies would be almighty cold.

And it was. And would have been colder still if Sandy Reese had stayed put in her own bedroll . . .

They broke camp early, eating cold hardtack and washing it down with stream water that tasted pure but was icy enough to numb a man's palate.

The peaks that rose above them, disappearing into low cloud cover, were heavy with residual snow, gleaming and glittering with its dampness.

'Thaw can't be far off,' Drayton opined as he followed the girl along a narrow, twisting trail that clung to the outer face of a jagged peak like a broken tooth.

'Just a matter of days,' she said, gasping a little in the thinner air up here. 'The wind may feel cold, but it's a good few degrees warmer than it was a week ago.'

'Don't like the way that snow just sort of hangs up there, poised like it's getting ready to fall . . .'

She hipped in the saddle, an amused look on her face. 'Don't tell me the great Buck Drayton is scared?'

'I'm not much for snow country,' he admitted. 'Seen a whole wagontrain of pilgrims lost under a snowslide once.' They rode on a bit further before he added, 'I was the guide and scouting on ahead when it happened.'

She frowned, threw him a sympathetic look but said nothing.

For quite some time as they climbed the twisting trail, the lower Medicine Bows now lost in mists below them, they seemed to be sandwiched between clouds above and fog below.

Then they topped-out on a rise and she halted, still breathing hard in the thin air as she waited for him to come up alongside. She pointed down and he saw below, on a wide ledge at the base of a snow-covered peak, several old weathered shacks, the slopes dotted with black holes that were actually the entrances to abandoned gold mines.

'Sierra High. That's what they called

the whole settlement. They say there were nearly two hundred men here at one time before they realized that it was just a freak vein that had made a half-dozen men rich and then petered out . . . '

Drayton nodded, feeling just a mite light-headed and as if there was an iron band tightening slowly about his chest. 'Never was much gold in this part of Wyoming. How come Landon chose here to hide-out?'

'I don't know . . . maybe he didn't have a choice.'

'How d'you mean?'

'I think Gunn sent him here. There're two or three men with him. Guards. They gave my girls a hard time when they came out here. But Gunn paid us well so I suppose there's nothing to complain about.'

'You'd be better changing professions, Sandy.'

She laughed shortly. 'You really believe that after last night . . . ?'

He felt himself flush and she laughed,

louder, and it echoed off the rocks. He put a hand on her arm and squeezed hard. She stopped abruptly, looking afraid, but the echoes drifted down into the ghost town below.

Drayton tightened his lips and eased his rifle out of the saddle scabbard as a man appeared in the door of the largest shack. He noticed now the thin streamer of blue woodsmoke coming out of the chimney.

'Damn! He's spotted us!'

'What're we going to do?' Sandy asked hoarsely.

'Hey! Art! That you?'

Drayton and the girl looked at each other and she said, 'He's mistaken you for Cregar! You're about his size, or a bit bigger! Wave back! He'll think I'm here for their comfort, too!' She waved vigorously, as Drayton gave a half-hearted lift of his free hand. Then she called, 'You better have some hot grub waiting for us, Swede!'

'I got more'n hot grub waitin'. That you, Sandy?'

169

'I'm too numb with cold to be sure, but I think so. You tell Zac I've got something special for him.'

'Hell with Zac! You just come on down! We'll show you a *special* good time!'

Two more men had appeared now as the girl led the way down, screening Drayton in part. One was a shortish man with broad shoulders and hair hanging down over his neck. The other was younger, taller, leaner, looked far less relaxed than the other two.

'Take your first look at Zac Landon,' Sandy said quietly as they started across the level part of the ledge towards the shack. 'The young one.'

Drayton slowed his gelding and the girl frowned as she looked at him sharply. 'Come on! They haven't realized yet you're not Cregar!'

'No — and that's not Zac Landon.'

Her frown deepened. 'I thought you'd never seen him?'

'Haven't — never saw Boy Daniels, either, but I saw a tintype of him —

and that's who that is, standing there with Gunn's guards: Boyce Jeremiah Daniels, J.D.'s pride and joy we all thought was dead and buried months ago.'

10

Sierra Stand-off

'You comin' on in or not?' shouted Swede as Drayton and Sandy Reese remained stationary in the faint mist now swirling in across the ledge.

'Be right there, Swede!' the girl called; then, to Drayton, 'We *have* to go in now! They'll get suspicious if we stop here.'

Drayton heeled his mount forward and Sandy put her horse in close alongside. He could hear the breath hissing through her nostrils and using the smoke's head for cover, quietly levered a shell into the breech of the Winchester which he carried across his thighs.

She squirmed uneasily.

Then Swede and the heavy-shouldered ranny with the long hair came forward, the latter hanging back a bit, one hand resting on his six-gun butt.

Drayton was waiting for it and a few moments later it came as the wide-shouldered man stopped dead, six-gun rising.

'*That ain't Cregar!*'

Swede moved like lightning, leaping to one side, dragging at his iron, even as Drayton's Winchester whiplashed and the wide-shouldered man staggered and fell to one knee. The used shell was still rising from the ejection port when the rifle cracked again and the man went down, grunting, but getting off two ragged shots. Sandy, white-faced, crouched low over her mount's neck and spurred off to one side.

The young man standing in the door of the cabin hadn't moved, but was watching closely, apparently unafraid of stray lead flying in his direction.

Swede was shooting and running across the ground, away from the big shack, making for the corner of another abandoned cabin with a tumbledown roof. His shots were wild and he zigzagged desperately as one of Drayton's bullets chewed splinters out of the corner post of the shack Swede was making for. He swung away, leaping backwards, shooting up at the big cowboy as he rode in on the smoke.

Swede yelled in panic, emptied his gun without a hope of hitting the man or horse and turned to run just as the smoke crashed into him. The impact sent him hurtling several feet and he hit the snow and slid and rolled wildly down the slope, out of control. His hands and boots left deep tracks in the snow but he had too much impetus to stop and a moment later he disappeared over the lip of an old mine shaft.

His scream echoed and dwindled until there was a crash of rotting timber followed by silence.

Drayton spun the steaming gelding back towards the cabin, seeing the wide-shouldered man sprawled unmoving in a patch of bloodstained snow, the girl stretched out along her mount against one wall. There was no sign of the young ranny.

Sandy made frantic gestures, telling Drayton that the man had gone back inside.

He dismounted, rifle at the ready as he made his way towards the open door. 'Boy? Name's Buck Drayton — J.D. sent me to find out what had happened to you. You've nothing to fear.'

No answer.

Drayton went in more warily, wondering if the man was getting a gun and already drawing a bead on him.

'Boy, there's a lot to talk about. Your pa thinks you're dead. So did I — until a few minutes ago. You can see I've got no truck with Gunn. Fact is, he could be somewhere along our back trail. It'll take him a long time to find any tracks but he might just assume we were heading here and come on in. You want to get out with a whole skin you'd best talk to me.'

Still no answer and Drayton edged closer, along the wall now, easing up to the door. Then Boy Daniels' voice said just the other side of the wall, 'You didn't come here to kill me?'

'I told you why I came. I'm a top hand on the Broken D. Your father sent me to find Landon and reward him for taking care of you . . . but it looks like we all had the wrong idea.'

Then Boy Daniels appeared in the doorway, holding his empty hands well out from his sides, making sure that Drayton could see he was unarmed.

'I'm a'wearyin' of the whole damn thing. I been freezin' my butt off up here for weeks. Come on in, Drayton. You too, Sandy!' he added, raising his voice.

Inside, the cabin was warm with flames leaping in an open fireplace. It didn't smell too clean, but that was to be expected with three hard men living here for weeks and with nowhere to go.

Daniels poured them coffee, but didn't have any for himself. He wasn't as young close up as he had looked while standing in the doorway, but Drayton knew he couldn't be more than thirty. His face was slightly scarred, bruised and cut, and he dragged one leg a little, seeming to favour the knee. His eyes disturbed Drayton, though. There was a wildness in them and a — a kind of *lethargy* — was the word he thought of though it didn't quite fit.

But it seemed to him that whatever it was it told anyone keen enough to spot it that here was a man who no longer cared about anything much in this life. Maybe he wasn't quite ready for suicide, but he sure wouldn't care about anyone else losing their life for whatever reason.

In Drayton's long experience of the hard life he'd led, this was one of the most dangerous signs in any man: total lack of feeling for any other human being.

Boy Daniels sat edgily on a chair, his fingers interlacing and undoing, tapping the table edge, or drumming on his thighs. Once he smiled at Sandy.

'I was hopin' you or one of your gals would show soon, Sandy.'

Sandy smiled. 'We had some good times, Zac — er — '

'Yeah, you can keep callin' me that — but it don't really matter now.'

'The real Landon in that grave at Medicine Bow?' Drayton asked and Daniels nodded.

'How much you know?'

He told him about his father's version of things and his own adventures since coming north to look for Daniels' body.

Boy Daniels nodded, his true focus far, far away from this old cabin in Sierra High. 'Knew I could fool Pa, but I never thought he'd send anyone to come a'lookin' for my grave. Shoulda reckoned on it, though, knowin' him.'

'Maybe he wouldn't've if he'd known about the payroll robbery.'

Daniels reared up in his chair, looking at Drayton almost in fear.

'*Judas!* Who the hell are you? You work for the army . . . ?'

Drayton lifted his six-gun casually and placed it on the table, nodding to Daniels' chair. 'Sit down, Boy. I've been lucky and I ran into Reuben Sadler — recollect him?'

Daniels sat slowly. 'Ol' Rube? He still alive? Hell, figured the lung disease would've took him long ago.'

'He's on his way to the Broken D now. With his family — but that part's no concern of yours at the moment. You want to tell us what happened?'

Daniels was quiet for a while, fetched them each more coffee then got a tobacco sack and papers from the end of one of the bunks. His fingers shook as he began to roll a cigarette.

'If you talked with Rube, you know me and Zac were kicked outa the army.' Drayton nodded. 'Well, Zac ain't here to defend himself, but it was all his idea. Gospel. He caught me just right. I'd lost my sergeant's stripes because of a brawl.' He rubbed at one temple,

179

frowning. 'Still get *these damn head-aches*! Had 'em since the end of the war . . . drive me crazy an' I just have to hit out at anything or anyone handy.'

'You can get treatment, Boy,' Drayton said quietly, and the man laughed briefly, lit his cigarette.

'Sure! While I'm on the run? Never mind. I gotta live with 'em an' that's all there is to it. Yeah, well, like I said, Zac struck me just right, said he had a few 'deals' that I could help with. I was reduced to 'wagoner' by then after they took my stripes and it weren't no trouble to smuggle the stuff he was sellin', dump it at a rendezvous and so on.'

'But you got caught, the army not being as dumb as you figured, and were court-martialled and sentenced to a labour camp.'

Daniels glared. 'All right! So you're another smart bastard, but the Injuns pulled a massacre or two and they lost interest in us long enough for us to break out. We were on the run and

180

broke and Zac said he knew the route the next pay train'd be takin' and all we needed was help to grab us a share and then we could head for South America.'

'You made contact with Milton Gunn?'

'Zac knew him — owed him money from gamblin'. That was Zac's big failin' — good ideas but chancy. This time he reckoned to square things away with Gunn. He said he'd back us with his men but — well, *hell*! I dunno why a man has to have so much blamed hard luck in his life!'

'That was what went wrong, was it? Just hard luck? Couldn't've been the army out-smarting fellers like you by having a troop ride out of sight but within gunshot of the pay train? Just in case . . . ?'

Daniels' face was really ugly now and Sandy gave a small gasp. 'Don't take to you, Drayton! Too much of a smart-ass . . . But, yeah, it all went wrong. Helluva battle.' He touched his face. 'Zac got burned when a wagon caught fire and fell on him. Men were shot down all over the place. I was hit twice and then Zac's hoss went off a cliff. Didn't find him for three days and he was mighty bad by then.'

Drayton frowned. '*Zac Landon* was the one all smashed up, not you? *You* nursed *him* through, but told your parents in that letter it was you who'd been nursed by Landon! The hell were you thinking of?'

Boy Daniels smiled crookedly. 'You mightn't believe it but I — cared for my parents. Knew Ma was poorly and not long for this world. The old man had been OK to me. It was one of them times I was free of headache and I — well, I didn't want 'em to get word of what I'd done. So I wrote that letter, made out I'd been wounded bad in a cavalry battle and that I was dyin'. That talk about givin' Zac a reward for nursin' me was all hogwash, just a cover-up, sort of. Then I sent that note in Zac's name, disguisin' my writin', to say — I'd died. Figured that'd be the

end of it. They'd accept that and still
— think — well of me.'

Drayton held his gaze to Boy's face
and saw now that the man's eyes were
softer, had lost that cold, uncaring look.
Maybe only briefly, but it *had* gone for
the moment. Just for now, he actually
cared about something. Just as he had
when he had written that letter.

'It was Zac who died, of course, and I
buried him in Medicine Bow. Afterwards I decided to take his name
— even put mine on that headboard.'

'But Gunn changed it to Landon's
when he set up Sandy here as Zac's
widow, to convince me Zac was dead.'

'That so? Well, that's all I gotta say.'

'Not by a long sight,' Drayton told
him quietly, his words bringing Daniels
twisting around, that dead look in his
eyes again.

The big cowboy indicated the cabin.
'What're you doing here? With two of
Gunn's men guarding you? Which
seems to me means that Gunn is
holding you here and he knows you

aren't really Landon, yet he told Sandy and her girls that's your name . . . I reckon there's plenty you haven't told us, Boy.'

Daniels sat down on the edge of a bunk now, and flicked the butt into the fire. 'Maybe I ain't gonna tell you!'

'Might as well,' Drayton said. 'Shouldn't matter to you what *we* think about you, a smart-ass cowboy and a whore — ' He caught Sandy's sharp look at that. He knew she wasn't insulted, not after all these years, but maybe she hadn't expected *him* to say it. 'We know the payroll robbery went all to hell, and we also know the money was never recovered — my guess is Gunn figures you know where it is . . . and he's keeping you handy until you tell him.'

Then he frowned. 'But why the hell would he wait all this time? Gunn doesn't strike me as a particularly patient man. His first reaction when he heard about me, was to send Cregar and Solomon out to kill me — '

Daniels started. 'And you got away! From *them*?'

Drayton ignored that. 'Then he thought better of it and set Sandy up as Zac Landon's widow to convince me Zac was dead. I already believed *you'd* died months ago.'

Daniels' eyes were narrowed as he watched Drayton.

'So, Gunn's kept you a prisoner here, under guard, and by the looks of things you've been beat up from time to time, which means he's been trying to get out of you where you stashed the payroll but you haven't told him . . . because you know you're dead once you do.'

'And maybe you've just got it backasswards!' Boy sneered.

Drayton raised his eyebrows, snapped his fingers.

'Or maybe he already *knows* where the payroll is but needs you to take him to it?' Drayton watched Daniels' face. It began to tighten, yet the man relaxed a little and curled a lip. Drayton spread his hands, one holding his six-gun just to remind Daniels who was in charge here. 'But I still don't get it. I can't figure out why he'd need you to guide him if he knows where it is.'

Daniels laughed, sounding genuinely pleased: the man's moods swung like an out-of-control pendulum the cowboy thought.

'Ah, you did pretty good, cowboy! Nearly got it, but not quite.'

Drayton waited. 'Well? You going to tell me?'

Daniels shrugged. 'Nah, don't think so ... I'm beginnin' to think it ain't worthwhile hangin' round any longer anyway. You killed Swede and Beef: I'm free now. Reckon it might be as well to settle for that and forget the goddamn payroll.'

Drayton didn't believe him for a second, asked casually, 'Just how much was it, anyway?'

'Seventy-five thousand doll — ' Daniels had automatically started to answer and now clamped his mouth shut and then cursed Drayton.

'No wonder Gunn's showing patience!' the cowboy said, glancing at Sandy whose eyes were bright at the mention of the payroll's worth. 'Even a man rich as he is would be prepared to wait a spell so as to get his hands on that much money.'

'Well, he ain't goin' to!' Daniels snapped, standing now — and he held a cocked six-gun trained on Drayton. He smiled crookedly. 'This was Swede's bunk. He always slept with a Colt under his pillow. Just keep your hands well away from that gun on the table, Drayton, but don't try to stand. I like you better sittin' down. Sandy, you just set still and keep your hands where I can see them.'

'All right, Zac,' she said a mite shakily. 'But I'm not in this, you know. I did what Gunn told me to — as usual — and I figured seeing as I was so close, in Medicine Bow, I might as well come up and keep you warm a couple of nights. Gunn didn't have to know. I like you, Zac, but he' — gestured to

Drayton — 'made me lead him here. Cregar and Oakey were to come with me but he came back and killed them.'

Daniels' eyes widened. 'Killed *Cregar*?'

She nodded, made a strangling motion with her slim hands. 'Fought him to a standstill and . . . ' Her hands opened and closed. 'He's a real scary son of a bitch, Zac . . . *real* scary.'

Daniels was rattled, all right. 'But Art Cregar was a — a snake! Lowest son of a bitch I ever met and tough as a grizzly. He done it *with his bare hands*?'

Sandy nodded and Daniels licked his lips, staring at Drayton. He seemed to be thinking for a spell then said, 'Reckon you're the kinda feller I'd like on *my* side, Drayton! I'm gonna need protection whatever I do . . . ' The man seemed to be thinking aloud now, rationalizing. 'If I run, Gunn's gonna send *someone* after me. Like that damn Mex, Raoul, an' he's near as bad as Cregar. Cowboy, how you like to earn yourself' — his lips moved as he did some sort of calculation — 'you could earn yourself somethin' over ten thousand dollars, if you stand between me an' Gunn.'

Drayton shook his head. 'Already working for your father, Boy.'

Daniels blinked. 'He can't be payin' you more'n that!'

'Nowhere near it, but I took the job and I'll see it through . . . for J.D.'

'You won't protect me from Gunn?'

'Didn't say that — I aim to take you back to Texas to J.D. He'll take you in whatever you've done, Boy. You're all he has now.'

'I don't *want* to go back to Texas! I'm a rich man now! I don't need J.D. He thinks I'm dead, let it stay that way! An' if you got notions any different to that and won't stand with me agin Gunn, then you ain't no use to me, cowboy!'

The six-gun came up and then there was a crack and Daniels yelled, twisting as he grabbed at his forearm, the gun thudding to the floor. Drayton kicked over the chair, leapt forward and hooked Daniels on the jaw. He caught the man as he staggered, rammed him down into a straightback chair and picked up the six-gun. He smiled at Sandy through the gunsmoke as she held the nickel-plated ladies' special he had returned to her back before they had left Medicine Bow.

'Just as well he didn't want to hop into the sack as soon as you arrived,' he said, smiling a little tightly. 'He'd have found the gun then.'

'You bitch!' Daniels snapped, looking at the bullet burn across his forearm.

'You ain't hurt bad,' Drayton said, standing in front of the chair now. 'Boy, you were offering me a share of that payroll which tells me you still aim to get your hands on it, no matter what you've been saying.'

'Yeah, and I'm the *only* one who can do it!'

Drayton eased his hips back against the table edge.

'I think I've got it figured now, Boy. You've been waiting for the thaw to start, haven't you?'

One look at Boy Daniels' shocked face was all the confirmation he needed.

'You either hid the money somewhere that's now covered by snow and can't be reached until it thaws, or you were caught by a snowslide that buried the payroll — and you *still* have to wait for it to thaw before you can reach it.'

Drayton glanced at Sandy Reese.

'That's why Gunn's been holding him here, waiting it out. It'd be the *only* reason he'd be so damn patient.'

They both watched Daniels whose shoulders were slumped now, Then he slowly tied a kerchief around his forearm which was bleeding slightly.

'All right. Yeah, Zac and me got away with the payroll in all the confusion after the attack by that guard troop we knew nothin' about. We waited at the rendezvous for Gunn's men to show up and they never did. So we figured we'd keep the payroll ourselves and make a run for it.'

'You said Zac Landon had been burned and badly hurt during the gun fight,' Drayton reminded him.

Daniels shook his head. 'No. Happened later. A grizzly come into one of our camps one night, ripped Zac up pretty bad, and he got burned in the fire. I emptied a six-gun and a shotgun into the damn bear, but the shootin' started a snow slide . . . I still dunno how I drug Zac out and got away . . . '

'So the payroll's buried. Or gone forever if an avalanche swept through your camp.'

'No. A *snowslide*! That's different. Hundreds of tons of snow dumped into the camp, which was on a ledge. It piled up to hell an' gone, but didn't spill over into an avalanche. We'd already stashed the money in a cave. Think now it must've been the bear's an' that's why he come stormin' into camp and ripped-up poor old Zac.'

'And you reckon you can find this cave again after the thaw?'

Daniels smiled thinly. 'One thing

that's never failed me, cowboy, and that's my sense of direction. I can go straight to it, soon as the snow thaws enough.'

'Well, you can't wait here,' Drayton told him. 'Gunn had someone trailing us and they'll turn up here eventually. You know anywhere else we can go?'

Daniels' eyes narrowed. 'Decided to cut yourself in now, have you?'

'Why not? Now I know you can find the money again.'

He avoided looking at Sandy who was watching him closely. She said, 'Well, I wouldn't mind a slice of it, too.'

'You take your cut out of Drayton's share!' Boy snapped. 'I ain't splittin' it no more ways!'

Sandy arched her eyebrows at Drayton and he nodded. 'I'll see you right, Sandy.'

'Then what're we waiting for?' she said, standing.

They were all preparing to move when a voice called from outside.

'You in there, Drayton? Reckon you

are with two of my best men dead out here. Come to the door. I want to show you something!'

'*Gunn!*' hissed Daniels, going white now.

Drayton, too, was surprised to hear Milt Gunn's voice and Sandy had to sit down, her legs suddenly weak.

Drayton took his six-gun and walked to a shuttered window, looked out through a crack in the warped timber — and swore bitterly.

He saw what Gunn wanted to show him.

The man had Evelyn Bridges roped to a horse at his side and was backed up by half-a-dozen men, including Raoul.

11

Higher and Higher

'Who's that woman?' asked Boy Daniels petulantly as he peered through the warped crack beside Drayton.

'Someone I thought was safely back in Cheyenne.'

'What're we going to do?' asked Sandy shakily.

Daniels answered that for her, but not in so many words. He strode to the door and before Drayton could stop him wrenched it open.

'Thank God you got here, Milt! It's Drayton and Sandy — we're comin' out . . . '

And he stepped outside quickly even as Drayton lunged for him. The cowboy stumbled and found himself halfway across the stoop, his gun in his hand, but under the cocked weapons of Milt

Gunn's crew. Evelyn Bridges watched, pale and obviously afraid. Boy hurried towards the group.

Milton Gunn looked quite pleased with himself, his face just visible within the wolf-fur hood of his heavy coat. 'Didn't think you'd be in such a hurry to see me again, Buck, or is it the young lady you're anxious about?'

'She's not in this, Gunn,' Drayton said, holstering his gun, knowing full well they would have all been happier if he had dropped the weapon in the snow. 'Let her go.'

'Bit late for that. She's served her main purpose in bringing you out, but I think I'll keep her around a little longer . . . long as I have her you'll stay in line.'

Drayton moved his gaze to Evelyn's white face. 'Sorry about this.'

'As Gunn just said, a bit late, Buck. But it's not your fault. Gunn has his own line of thinking.'

The gambler laughed shortly. 'She's something, isn't she? Always had a soft spot for Evelyn, even when she wrote me up as being a bad guy. Sent her flowers but never got me even close. Maybe a few days on the slopes here will change her mind.'

'Let her go now, Gunn, and I won't kill you,' Drayton said mildly.

The words caused a little stirring amongst the armed men and Gunn arched his eyebrows. 'Knew you had plenty of gall, Buck, but you're a long way from killing me or anyone else. Fact, you'd do better to worry about yourself and never mind Evelyn. I'll take care of her.'

Drayton said no more, but Gunn found himself shifting a little uneasily in the saddle at the look in Drayton's eyes: he knew at that moment that the big man *would* kill him at the first opportunity.

And the big cowboy would *make* the opportunity or give it a damn good try . . .

Gunn, angry with himself, turned to Boy Daniels.

'It's about time you showed me where that payroll is.'

'Hell, Milt, look at the snow still banked up!'

'It's melting. Water's pouring down the slopes, dripping from all those ledges.'

'Yeah, it's the start of the thaw,' admitted Daniels, 'but there's a long ways to go. Best part of a week, I'd say.'

Gunn glanced sidelong at Raoul and the Mexican jumped his mount forward, knocking the startled Daniels to the ground. As he rolled and tried to get up, Raoul walked his mount forward and over him, surrounding him by the stomping hoofs. Daniels instinctively covered his head with his arms, starting to yell. But that only made the horse more nervous and Boy shouted as a hoof caught one arm, ripping a large chunk out of his sheepskin jacket sleeve. Blood flowed as he snatched the arm across his chest. On his back he worked his legs frantically, sliding out from under the horse.

But, as he started up, Raoul, dark eyes glittering, enjoying this, rammed his mount into him again. Daniels went down hard, was slower to roll away. The horse came after him, Raoul getting ready to rear it up on its hind legs.

Drayton lunged forward, hit the side of the horse hard, setting it off-balance just as it started to rear. At the same time he yanked Raoul's left boot free of the ornate stirrup and heaved the man out of the saddle.

He hit hard, rolling, snatching at his gun. Drayton stomped on his gun hand, pinning it to the frozen ground, grinding with his boot. The deerskin gloves shredded and Raoul bared his teeth as he groaned and bit back against the pain. The hand was useless now, couldn't hold the gun, as the Mexican staggered to his feet, face white with rage and pain.

Gunn heeled his own horse forward and clubbed Drayton to his knees with his six-gun butt. Raoul leapt in, kicking, raking with his spurs. Drayton was conscious enough to shield his face, but his jacket sleeve was torn open from elbow to wrist. He rolled away and Raoul sprang after him, reaching for his knife.

But a sharp command from Gunn stopped him and the man contented himself with another kick at Drayton and then tore off his fancy silk neckerchief and wrapped it around his smashed hand. His eyes were filled with hate and death.

'You're a dead man, cowboy,' Milt Gunn said affably enough. 'I won't be able to hold him back for long.'

Drayton was groggy, swayed on his feet, rubbing at the knot on the back of his head. He said something, but the words were too slurred to be intelligible.

'Let's get in out of this cold,' Gunn said abruptly. 'You men pick yourself a cabin to sleep in ... Raoul, you stay with me.'

Raoul smiled thinly.

There was no way that the Mexican

was going to let Drayton out of his sight.

Evelyn was detailed to take care of Raoul's broken hand and she bathed it in hot water, but there were no medicines so all she could do was bind it with strips torn from a flour sack and make a sling. The Mexican bit into his lips at the pain until beads of blood showed. But he didn't utter another sound.

Only glared and glared at Drayton.

Evelyn also tended Buck's arm that had been cut by Raoul's spur rowels and Daniels' arm which was badly bruised and cut from the horse's hoof. Two armed men leaned against the wall just inside the door. Gunn hogged the fire and Daniels sat sullenly on his bunk. Sandy sat silent and tense on another of the empty bunks.

'We start up the mountain tomorrow morning,' Gunn announced. He looked towards Boy. 'How long will it take us to reach this cave where you say the money's stashed? And it *better had be* stashed like you say!'

'It's there, Milt, I swear it,' Daniels said. 'But it's too soon to go up there. The cave entrance kind of slants inwards and there's a thousand tons of snow piled above it. Went up a coupla days ago while Swede and Beef were asleep. It's startin' to melt, but it'll be at least a week before it's safe to go up there.'

Gunn heaved to his feet with a sigh, walked across to where Daniels sat and backhanded him casually.

'I've waited long enough! You and Landon blew the whole deal and it's time you squared it away!'

Daniels rubbed at his face. 'Milt, for Chris'sakes, I came to you in the first place! I coulda been halfway to Canada, but I came to you — '

'Because you needed my help and knew damn well you could traipse all the way to Alaska, but I'd catch up with you sooner or later.'

Boy Daniels nodded. 'Yeah, well — it's too dangerous to go up there yet.

Footing's too unsteady, slippy, wet, there's snow slides . . . '

Gunn hit him again. 'We start tomorrow. We can find somewhere safe to camp if it gets too dangerous, but *we go tomorrow!*'

He looked at Sandy Reese, sitting very stiffly and quiet on the edge of her bunk. 'Don't look to be many blankets on that bunk, Sandy, you can keep me warm, OK?'

Sandy nodded, smiled, but it was tight about the edges. Drayton knew she was afraid. Gunn had almost totally ignored her since his arrival, but sooner or later he was going to demand to know why she had brought Drayton here.

'Hope you have better luck than me,' Drayton said suddenly, bringing all eyes swinging towards him. 'I could twist her arm and make her bring me up here, but damned if I could get her into my bedroll.'

He avoided looking at Evelyn but saw the relief and gratitude in Sandy's eyes as he tried to get her off the hook with Gunn. She tilted her jaw at him.

'Told you, Texas. I'm fussy who I sleep with when I'm not working!'

It pleased Gunn and he laughed outright.

Drayton only hoped it had worked to allay his suspicions that Sandy might have willingly brought him to Boy's hideout.

* * *

It was a clear but bitterly cold morning. A wind straight from the icecap blew across the ledge and turned Sierra High into a freezebox.

None of them, including Gunn, were eager to leave the warmth of the cabins but Gunn was a man who once he had said he would do something, did it.

So, miserable with cold and ungainly in all the heavy clothing they wore, the group set out, Boy Daniels riding on ahead with Gunn and Raoul flanking him. Drayton saw the Mexican slide his injured hand from the sling and work the fingers awkwardly. He could not fit a glove on the swollen digits and Evelyn had wrapped extra layers of bandages around them to keep out the cold.

But it was plain to Drayton that the Mexican was attempting to get his gun hand in working order again. Not that he really needed it for killing: Drayton expected an attempt to cut his throat, or a knife blade in the kidneys, or between the shoulders. Or maybe the man would simply push him over a cliff. But the attempt *would* come.

Sooner or later Raoul was going to try to kill him whether Gunn sanctioned the move or not.

They had taken his six-gun of course, and he felt mighty naked despite his layers of clothing riding with this bunch. Evelyn rode alongside, but Gunn kept Sandy up front with him. The other half-dozen gunmen were scattered down the line, two close to Drayton, the other four bringing up the rear.

By mid-morning the wind had dropped considerably and the sun was shining though there was little warmth in it as yet. Even so, some of the layered snow on ledges and covering rocks began to take on a wet glitter and drops formed, though they tended to extend into icicles rather than dripping free. But an hour later it had started: even above the sounds of the blowing mounts and the crunch of snow and gravel underfoot, they could all hear it blanketing the mountain.

Myriad drips at first then blending into trickles, and, as the sun grew stronger, the trickles became rivulets, the rivulets tiny streams cutting through the snow that had lain there all winter and this far into spring. The water, crystal clear at first, soon became muddied and slushy underfoot. Hooves slipped and skidded. Horses snorted, steam enveloping their tossing heads.

There was a narrow trail where it wasn't safe for two riders to stay alongside each other. Boy Daniels argued with Gunn that it was too dangerous to travel at this time, with all the slush and the snow falling in dollops.

'A horse puts a foot wrong he's gone,' Boy said, jerking a head towards the long drop down to the rugged lower slopes.

'We'll dismount and walk 'em through,' Gunn said, and, hipped in saddle without awaiting a reply, giving the order.

'And keep an eye on Drayton!'

'Last time I looked, I didn't have wings growing out of my back,' Drayton said but Gunn ignored him.

The horses didn't like it, balking, snorting, taking a lot of coaxing. Two of the gunmen behind Drayton cuffed their mounts with their hats, cursing and kicking the forelegs.

Drayton stood it for as long as he could.

'You'll never make progress like that,' Drayton snapped, turning to lend a hand.

'Who asked you, Texas!' demanded the nearest man and raised his quirt to lash at the big cowboy.

Drayton covered fast and lurched — maybe his boots slipped in the slush — but he fell into the man and suddenly the gunman was screaming and flapping his arms wildly as he turned end over end in space, dropping quickly from sight.

The man behind him shouted, 'You done that a'purpose!' and tried to get past the falling man's mount which was skittish and backing around.

A moment later the second man was falling, too, but he yelled curses all the way down . . .

The group had halted and there was sudden silence as the dying echoes faded.

'Shoot him!' snapped Gunn, pointing to Drayton.

But as the men levered cold rifles, Evelyn stepped in front of the cowboy, looking wildly at Gunn.

'No! He did nothing! He was trying

to help that first man when he was attacked and fell against him! The other man tried to get to him but the horse was frightened and knocked him off the trail! It was accidental! I *saw* it!'

Gunn's men looked at him for further orders and he stared sullenly at the cowboy and the woman for what seemed a long time but in reality was no more than a few seconds.

'All right — this time I believe you. If there's another such incident, you'll both be shot on the spot!'

The men looked disappointed as they got moving again. Drayton moved close to Evelyn. 'Thanks.'

'I don't know what really happened,' she said, a bit tensely.

He looked straight into her questioning eyes. 'Just the way you told it,' he said, deadpan, and she held his gaze a moment longer, then nodded.

'Of course.'

He couldn't tell if she was convinced or not.

* * *

By noon they were well above the ledge of abandoned gold mines and still climbing, although the steepness wasn't so bad now, the trail meandering across the face of the sierra.

There were roaring streams all over the mountain slope now and they were forced to discard some of their clothing, or open up their jackets. Soon the afternoon wind would start up again and it would be a mighty cold camp this night, but it was quite warm at this time, due mainly to their exertions.

Boy Daniels, breathing raggedly at this altitude, stopped on a rocky bench that had several small waterfalls pouring off it that would no doubt freeze tonight into spectacular daggers of ice, until the sun started the thaw again in the morning. He waited for Gunn to come closer and leaned back, pointing above.

'That's where we're going to have trouble. See that snowbank on the jutting slope? It leans out above where we'll have to travel. It's too thick and too high to have thawed much yet, but if the wind doesn't start up, the sun'll warm that slope early — and there's a thousand tons of snow just waitin' to slip off and come down on us.'

Gunn looked at the snow and then at Boy. 'You're doing your best to keep us from reaching this cave where you reckon the money is, Boy — '

Daniels shook his head quickly. 'No, Milt! I'm not makin' excuses! See for yourself! Anyone with half a brain can see it's — '

Gunn's hand smashed him across the narrow face, staggering him. Boy blinked and tasted blood, felt a loosened tooth with the tip of his tongue.

'I — I'm sorry, Milt!' he slurred. 'I — I didn't mean it that way. All I meant was that you can *see* how it's just kinda hangin' there! We oughta get off this slope for the night at least.'

Gunn seemed to think about it,

looked around the bench, decided the rocks would give them good shelter from any wind that might spring up and agreed that they would make camp, but back at where the bench first began, amongst the rocks and out of line of any avalanche that might start.

'Not that I figure it will,' he added, staring hard at Boy. 'But we better get to where we're going tomorrow or *someone's* gonna be buried in the snow, avalanche or not.'

Boy swallowed. 'If there ain't too much wind or melt-water, we — we oughta be there by this time tomorrow.'

'Not *oughta*, Boy! We *will* be, and we'll be counting the money tomorrow night around the camp-fire. Or you'll have seen your last sunrise!'

Daniels seemed really worried and Gunn set him to helping Drayton and Evelyn unload the firewood from the pack horses and prepare the fire and food for camp.

'We gonna make the deadline?' Drayton asked Boy.

Boy half-turned, hunkered down as he poked at the fire. Then he sat back on his hams and rubbed violently above his right eye.

'I dunno,' he said in a growling tone. 'And the way this goddamn headache's workin'-up I don't care one way or t'other.'

'Well, I reckon I do.'

'Your tough luck . . . now get away from me. You're nothin' but trouble.'

'I do my best,' Drayton said and moved over to help Evelyn cut some venison steaks from the haunch they had brought from Sierra High.

'What's wrong with Boy?'

'Headache. He's scared, though. Dunno whether it's Gunn or the thought of an avalanche.'

She looked at him quickly. 'I — I don't feel exactly relaxed and at ease myself.'

He nodded. 'I think Gunn would've done better to listen to Boy but he's grown too impatient.'

'Too greedy, you mean. Why did Boy

213

take Landon's name when his own was already on the headboard?'

'Likely Gunn's idea. He knew he was going to have to hide Boy until the thaw and he'd need to keep him more or less happy, too — like sending in women . . . '

'Whores, you mean? Like Sandy?'

Drayton nodded. 'Better if they didn't know the name 'Boy Daniels'. Gunn didn't know much about J.D., but he's a man who respects power and he'd heard enough to know J.D. wields a good bit of that down Texas way.'

'And he changed the name on the headboard to Zac Landon — ironically, seeing as it's the correct one. But why?'

Drayton shrugged.

'Because when he found out I'd been sent up to find Landon to give him a reward, he had Sandy pose as Landon's widow to convince me there was nothing left to look for so I'd go back. Even if Boy's name had been on the headboard, I was still s'posed to find Landon.'

'Were you too smart for them, or just too stubborn?'

He smiled thinly. 'Stubborn. J.D. put his trust in me. I owe it to him to find out exactly what happened.'

'Even if it gets you killed?'

'Well, I wasn't planning on that . . . '

He grunted and sprawled as one of the gunmen kicked him savagely in the side, stretching him out on the ground.

'Shut up and get that grub cooked!' The man leaned down towards him. 'You pushed my two pards off that high trail today, no matter what you say! When it comes time to kill you, I'm gonna be there, Drayton.'

Drayton grunted, holding his side as he struggled to sit up. 'Better — stand — in — line.'

The man cuffed him and moved away.

Sandy Reese was still being kept close to Gunn, but she looked towards Drayton and Evelyn now, teeth tugging at her lower lip. Raoul leaned against a

215

rock out of the wind which was springing up, arms folded, glaring at Drayton.

Supper was a silent affair, the only words spoken were by Gunn and his men demanding more food or coffee.

Afterwards, the prisoners were bound hand and foot and that included Boy Daniels much to his displeasure.

It was a cold, uncomfortable night for everyone and Drayton heard Gunn and Sandy arguing, the girl trying to get him to change his mind and go back down the mountain.

'I don't like it up here, Milt. I'm scared of all that snow just hanging to the slopes above us. The thaw is the most dangerous time to be in the Sierras, everyone knows that. Please let me go back! You don't need me here, Milt!'

'Just shut up and go to sleep.'

'But we can wait down at Sierra High until the snow melts off the slopes and it's safe to go up for the money. For

Chris'sakes, Milt! Send *me* back if you don't want to come! But *I want to get off this damn mountain*!'

There came the sound of a hard slap and sobbing and Gunn's bad-tempered voice.

'One more word and you'll get off the mountain all right! Straight over the goddam side! Now — *go to sleep*!'

★ ★ ★

They were having breakfast when they heard a sound like distant thunder and Sandy Reese, her face swollen and lop-sided, looked at Gunn with wide eyes.

'What's that?'

'Storm blowing up, I guess,' he said casually.

Drayton didn't know if the man was really ignorant of the true cause of the thunder-like sound, or if he was deliberately lying.

But *he* knew what that sound meant: it was the first snow slide caused by the

217

thaw, the huge weight of the snow on the wet, steep slopes unable to retain its hold any longer.

The whole mountain was getting ready to move.

12

'Don't Shoot!'

During the night, the wind had dropped and there was no more than an icy breeze come sun-up and even that fell away after an hour.

The sun held little warmth at first, a pale glow through clouds and ground mist. Then these burned away and the sky showed clear and brilliantly blue and sunlight washed over the lower slopes. The deep snow banks on the higher slopes had been receiving warmth for more than an hour.

The constant dripping of the thawing snow over rocks and ledges became a low background sound, like the aftermath of a heavy rainstorm. Slush began to slide down the steep slopes. Dollops of snow rimmed with ice spilled off precarious perches where it could no longer grip. It fell in chunks from the black naked branches of the few scattered trees here above the timber-line.

The mountain was on the move.

As they broke camp, none of them could stop thinking about all those thousands of tons of snow perched above on the high slopes where they were going.

Drayton, his hands roped to the saddlehorn, weaved his mount through the strung-out guards and rode up alongside Gunn, Raoul at the ready with drawn knife and eager expression. Gunn lifted a hand, staying any move he might have been going to make.

'Problem, cowboy?'

'We're heading up to snow that's had the sun warming it for a lot longer than the stuff down here. Just listen to that rushing water. *Look* at it!' He jerked his head in the direction of two foaming, chocolate-coloured streams of surging melt-water a hundred yards to the right. When the water hit the ledges, small waterfalls formed, this water carving deep channels in the snow below, carrying small rocks and gravel and a few deadfall branches with it as it churned on downslope.

Gunn set his cold gaze on Drayton. 'Don't be such an old lady. We delay any longer and we'll have the whole damn mountain coming down on us. We can get to the cave and out again today, if we push it a little.'

'You're crazy. Hell, it's only money, Gunn.'

The gambler's eyes narrowed and he flicked them towards Raoul. Drayton started to turn but something smashed across his head, knocking his hat askew, sending the world into a spin. Another painful blow rattled his spine. A third sent white-hot needles of pain through his kidneys.

Only the ropes held him in the saddle as he sagged to one side, hurting deeply, senses spinning.

Gunn's tightly smiling face was a blur.

'Drayton, I came along in person because I figured any man who could kill Art Cregar hand-to-hand had to be someone to reckon with. Now I'm not so sure just why I've kept you around this long. Just for now, consider you're living on borrowed time. But — you do *exactly* like I say, else Sweet Evelyn won't look so pretty . . . '

'Uh,' was the best that Drayton could manage.

'Now get back into line and don't approach me again. If you do, Raoul has permission to shoot.'

For the first time since having his gunhand broken, the Mexican smiled.

'Christ, don't shoot!' said Boy Daniels, who had witnessed the whole incident. As all eyes turned to him, he added, 'A gunshot triggered the slide that buried the cave. We oughtn't even *talk* loud! We could bring the whole damn mountain down on top of us.'

Milt Gunn stared at Boy for a long time. 'You're a damn Nervous Nellie and I've had about a bellyful of you.

You been stalling me for months — now get back up front and keep climbing . . . *I want that money today!*'

Sullenly, looking worried, Daniels turned his mount, his shoulders stiff. He raised one hand to his forehead and rubbed it above his right eye. Sandy Reese looked very pale, her teeth chewing at her bottom lip as she watched the increasing number of muddy streams carving up the slopes.

Evelyn — for some reason her hands had not been tied to the saddlehorn this morning — rode forward, took the bridle of Drayton's mount and led him back to his position in the line. Almost everyone had an apprehensive look.

'You're going to be so beat-up,' Evelyn told Drayton quietly, 'that even if there is a chance to make a run for it, you'll be in no shape to take it.'

Drayton smiled tightly through his pain. 'There's already a chance.'

The girl was startled. 'What? With all these armed men?'

'Uh-huh — and unless they're even

dumber than I think, they won't dare shoot, not after what Boy said. Did you see Gunn's face? He covered pretty well, but he's worried, all right.'

'Shut up, you two!' snapped the nearest guard, a lean man with Oriental features whom everyone called Chan.

Drayton turned as far as his ropes would allow him. 'I was just saying, Raoul must've busted something loose in my kidneys — I need to go bad.' He nodded to a big black boulder. 'Over there'd do.'

Chan hawked and spat, then as Drayton grimaced and doubled over, called, 'Hey, boss! Drayton says he's bustin' to take a piss!'

His loud voice echoed around the slopes and every rider in the group hauled rein, swinging to look at Chan.

'Keep your voice down, you idiot!' hissed Gunn, his eyes blazing.

Chan swallowed worriedly. 'Sorry, boss,' he said, much more quietly.

Gunn didn't say anything, only waved the riders on. Most of the men, and Sandy Reese, were watching the slopes above. Chan said cheerfully, 'Looks like you'll have to go in your pants, Drayton!'

The cowboy said nothing, but Evelyn watched his face and then, ignoring the guards, weaved her mount closer to Gunn. Raoul put his horse between her and the gambler who waited for her to speak.

'Buck's in real pain, Milt. There's a danger his kidneys are bruised and who knows what might happen unless the pressure on them is relieved.'

'If it gets bad enough he can pee in his pants, Evelyn.'

'And then he'll freeze and be no good for anything — least of all to send into a cave after your money.'

Gunn was sober now. 'I know you're smart, Evelyn, your journalism has proved that many a time — you're trying to manipulate me.'

'I'm merely stating facts, Milt. That man's really suffering!'

'*Bueno!*' said Raoul with a wide grin.

Gunn glared, then said abruptly, 'Raoul, go cut the cowboy loose, but you stay with him and tie him up again soon's he's finished.'

The knife was already in Raoul's hand. 'I cut *something* for him!'

'Just the ropes!' Gunn snapped.

The Mexican pushed Evelyn roughly aside with his horse, rode back to Drayton.

He snatched the smoke's bridle. It fought a little and he cursed as he led Drayton across to the big boulder and behind it, out of sight of the others.

Raoul hammered his good hand into Drayton's lower back and the cowboy slumped forward with a groan as the *cuchillo* blade slashed the ropes holding him to the horn. Drayton tumbled to the slushy ground and lay there, gasping, drawing his knees up in pain. The severed ropes dangled from the saddlehorn and he worked his numbed hands briefly.

Raoul waved the knife, the blade

glittering in the sunlight. '*Pees*, Drayton! And I hope it hurts!'

The cowboy gritted his teeth and grabbed the stirrup to drag himself upright. He fell against the smoke, panting. 'I *know* it'll hurt, you greaser son of a bitch!'

Raoul dismounted quickly and came striding across the slope, slipping slightly, knife ready for a belly stroke. Then Drayton snatched the severed ropes that still had the knot tied in one end and slashed the man across the eyes.

The Mexican jerked, his boots slipping, and he fell, instinctively putting down his bad hand to break the fall. A moan of pain was wrenched out of him as the hand folded under his weight and then Drayton was on him, kicking the knife out of reach, driving a knee into that cruel, narrow face.

Raoul fell back in the mud and only raging hatred drove him on through extreme pain as he lifted a boot and raked at Drayton's belly with the big spur. The rowel ripped his heavy jacket. He snatched the boot, twisted hard, wrenching the ankle. It spun the Mexican on to his face and he slid backwards a few feet, good hand groping for the knife which lay somewhere in the mud and slush.

Drayton rammed a knee savagely into the man's spine and Raoul made a choking sound. The cowboy repeated the blow and the Mexican twisted away sickly, kicking out. A spur raked across Drayton's shin and stopped him in his tracks. The wiry Mexican climbed shakily to his feet and fumbled out his six-gun with his left hand.

Panting, standing all straddle-legged for balance, Drayton bared his teeth. 'Go ahead, Raoul! Pull the trigger and bring down the mountain!'

Raoul *wanted* to shoot, very badly, but he recalled Boy's words as he started to cock the hammer. Then Drayton slipped and went down on one knee. He scooped a handful of slush and flung it into Raoul's face.

The Mexican reared up and Drayton dived for his gun arm, twisting the Colt free. His hands were slippery with mud and the weapon fell as both men crashed to the ground. Raoul tried to bite Drayton's ear off and the cowboy rammed a forearm across the man's throat. The Mexican coughed and choked, his groping hand finding a rock half-covered in slush. He brought it up and across as Drayton moved in and it took the man on the shoulder, numbing his arm clear down to the fingertips.

Teeth bared in triumph, Raoul threw himself at Drayton, the rock raised murderously. Then Drayton's left hand touched the *cuchillo* lying in the covering of mud. He snatched it up, hurled it swiftly and the blade buried itself to the hilt in the advancing Mexican's chest.

Raoul stopped dead, a look of surprise on his face, the rock falling from his hand. He went over backwards, his clawed hand dragging the knife out of his bleeding chest. Mud sprayed as Raoul sprawled with arms spread, dark, twisted face going slack as the life gushed out of him.

Gasping, body racked with pain, Drayton searched for the six-gun, found it and saw that it was going to have to be cleaned of mud before it would shoot. He got to his feet, caught Raoul's mount and slid the rifle from the saddle scabbard.

He whirled as he heard a horse coming: Gunn was sending someone to see what was keeping him. He levered a shell into the breech as Chan appeared, hauling rein sharply.

'Judas priest!' he exclaimed when he saw Raoul, then recovering, he sneered at Buck Drayton. 'You ain't gonna shoot!'

'You've got three seconds to decide if I will or not.' Drayton sounded quite casual, in control.

Chan ran a tongue across his lips and began to sweat despite the chill. Suddenly, he swung down from the saddle and raised his hands shoulder high, watching warily as Drayton moved towards him. 'Take it easy, friend!'

'Shuck your gunbelt,' the cowboy ordered and as Chan obeyed, stepped behind the man and crashed the butt of the rifle against the back of his head. Chan sprawled, sliding several feet downslope.

Drayton mounted his horse and rode around the boulder, rifle in hand. Gunn had halted the line and the riders stared in disbelief as he came into view, rifle covering them. He lifted the gun to his shoulder, drawing a bead on Gunn.

'Send the ladies back down the trail, Milt.'

Gunn scoffed. 'What're you going to do if I don't? Shoot me?'

'Right between the eyes,' Drayton told him coldly and Gunn's face straightened quickly.

'You'd never risk it!'

'What've I got to lose? I turn the gun over to you and I'm dead. Might as well take a chance on starting an avalanche.

231

But you won't know anything about it: the bullet's got your name on it, Gunn!'

The gambler swallowed. Everyone was sitting tensely, unmoving. Evelyn and Sandy stared at Drayton, wide-eyed. Boy Daniels looked pale, rubbed at his forehead, squinting.

'All right!' Gunn said breathlessly. 'They can go — '

Sandy turned her horse immediately and started to ride back down the narrow trail, throwing Drayton a quick look that could have meant anything: she was badly scared.

'What about you, Buck?' Evelyn asked, hesitating.

'Just get going, Evelyn — I'll catch up later.'

She still hesitated, then nodded, said a quiet, '*Thank you, Buck*,' then moved down the trail after Sandy.

After the women had disappeared around a bend, Gunn snapped, 'I think you've left yourself out on a limb, cowboy.'

'I'm still the one holding the rifle on

you, Milt.' Drayton looked at Daniels. 'You've waited a long time for this, Boy. You want to go get that money, or quit when you're within spitting-distance of becoming rich?'

'You're not going to let *him* walk away with that payroll!' Gunn demanded, shocked.

'Haven't decided yet, Milt. What d'you say, Boy? Turn back or go get it?'

Daniels seemed undecided.

'That's *my* money, damn you!' Gunn snarled.

'No, damnit!' Boy shouted, immediately cringing and lowering his voice as he glanced upwards — as did the others. 'Listen, no one's takin' that money from me! I've waited too long!'

He wheeled his mount and set off up the trail . . .

Drayton grinned at Gunn. 'You're gonna have trouble keeping your share, Milt.'

'That'll be the day!' Gunn growled and Drayton ordered them all to shuck their guns and when they had reluctantly obeyed they started up the trail after Boy Daniels.

* * *

It was another hour's climb before they found Daniels waiting by a steep slope with an overhang where glistening white snow clung in a layer several feet thick. They were all feeling the effects of the altitude and Boy said breathlessly, 'Top of the cave's showin'.' He pointed to a steep slope of melting snow. Above it protruded a ragged segment of a dark circle, part of the entrance to the cave.

He was squinting badly now and kept shaking his head. Drayton figured the high altitude was making the man's headache worse. He seemed very jumpy.

'Coupla more hours we ought to be able to get inside,' he told them.

Trying to take over again, Gunn said, 'That snow's soft — you can dig a hole big enough to get in.'

Boy glanced at Drayton who still held the rifle.

'Likely he's right, Boy. The quicker the sooner . . . ' He hitched around to look at the remaining three guards. 'Go give him a hand, fellers.'

They hesitated, then dismounted, climbed and floundered up the slope of snow and began digging alongside Boy, all using their hands. Gunn glanced at Drayton.

'That's *still* my money in there, cowboy.'

'Army might think different.'

'Hell with them. They'll have written it off long ago. I financed Boy and that fool Landon . . . I want a return on my investment. And I aim to get it.'

He smoothed out his tone when Drayton said nothing, sounded more reasonable, less bossy. 'Look, cowboy, considering everything, I've treated you pretty damn well.'

Drayton laughed shortly. 'Sure you have, Milt. Sent Big Art and Pres Solomon to bushwhack me. When that didn't work, you set up Sandy as Landon's fake widow, turned loose your damn Mex on me so I'll be lucky to ever take a piss again without gritting my teeth . . . yeah, you've done plenty for me, Milt. I don't think I'll ever forget it.'

Milton Gunn swallowed, moved uncomfortably, glanced at the four men labouring at the cave mouth.

It was slow, heavy work, this high up. Gunn was edgy and twice Drayton thought the man was desperate enough to try to grab the rifle from him but the gambler wasn't quite *that* game.

'We're through!' gasped one of the guards suddenly, as the last barrier of snow gave way. He pushed back quickly, coughing. 'Man! Smells like a grizzly's armpit in there!'

Even standing outside, Drayton could detect the strong animal smell coming from inside the cave.

'I've got matches,' Boy said, floundering forward.

'Go in with him!' Gunn snapped at his men.

But none of the guards would have it and Daniels slid down through the snow and moments later they saw the flare of his match as Boy went deeper into the cave.

There was silence, those outside scarcely breathing.

A few large dollops of snow about the size of a horse's head plopped from the snowbank above the cave, making Gunn jump. 'Hurry it up, Boy!' he shouted automatically.

'Not too loud, Milt,' Drayton cautioned, a trace of amusement in his words.

But the guards were worried. One of them said, 'See that? It's startin' to move!'

'So'm I!' said the man next to him and began to run for his horse. His companion followed but the third man glanced at Gunn first, started, then hesitated and finally stood still at the murderous look on the gambler's face.

The other two hit their saddles quickly and spurred wildly down the slushy trail, no longer interested in money, only in living a little longer . . .

Then Gunn, Drayton and the guard turned to the cave as Boy came slogging out to the entrance, only his upper body showing above the snow still banked across the opening.

He looked grim, his face skull-like and Drayton knew his headache was mighty bad.

'Hurry it *up*, will you!' demanded Gunn, walking forward.

Boy shook his head. 'No hurry. None at all now.'

Gunn stopped in his tracks. 'The hell're you saying?'

Boy's left hand moved and something rose above his head and then started to drift down like a snowfall, except the flakes were a faded green.

'What — what's that stuff?' Gunn asked hoarsely.

'The money! All that's left of the goddamn *money*!' Boy said, the words catching in his throat as the tiny scraps of paper wavered down to the snow. 'I've waited *months* and all I've got is — *this*!'

'What happened, Boy?' Drayton asked quietly, the others still stunned, staring.

'Pack rats. Cave must've been full of them. Starvin' all winter, I guess. Ate clear through the leather satchels, paper money and all . . . Only thing that's left is a coupla hundred bucks in silver dollars! And *they've* got teeth marks on them!'

His voice began to rise as his excitement increased and he stepped up onto the snow bank and they saw for the first time that he was holding a sawn-off shotgun. The barrels were glistening with oil so Drayton knew it must have been stowed in some durable container, left there when Boy and Landon had stashed the money. The hammers clicked back smoothly and Gunn started to back away, pushing a hand out palm-first towards Daniels.

'Take it easy, Boy! Don't you shoot that thing off here!'

'Hell, you think I care what happens now?' Boy sounded very down and totally apathetic. 'All my plans gone to hell! Thanks to you, Gunn!' His eyes were wild, crazy.

The gambler jumped, breathing hard now. 'Easy, kid . . . anyone's the loser here it's me! I financed you and Landon. You were the ones pulled the doublecross! Don't you go blamin' me for your troubles.'

'Back off, Gunn!' Drayton said sharply, seeing how close Boy was to the edge. He reached out for Gunn's shoulder to pull him back and suddenly Gunn whirled, grabbing at the rifle. They swayed, fighting for possession and then Gunn head-butted Drayton, staggering him. Gunn wrenched the rifle free and swung back towards Boy with a whine, in total panic now, fumbling at the lever.

The shotgun's barrels roared in a crashing thunder and the double charge of buckshot picked up Gunn's body, shredded it, and hurled him into the snow, red mixing with the white and brown.

The echoes slapped across the mountains. None of the three men still on their feet were breathing. They all looked up towards the steep, snow-covered slope above the cave as the echoes died and there was a strange, crushing silence.

Then they heard the sound they had been dreading.

A tearing, creaking groan as the snowcap loosened breaking the grip of a thousand tons of sun-warmed snow crystals.

It started to pour over the ledge, piling up at an incredible rate. Boy was already fighting to get free as it buried him up to the chest. In another second he was gone forever. The snow swept on like a huge smoking white wave, carrying Gunn's body across the ledge. The guard was running for his horse when the wall caught him, and the mount as well. Any sound was drowned by the thunder of the mountain on the move and guard and horse disappeared.

Drayton leapt into the smoke's saddle, fighting the terrified animal around, raking with his spurs, urging it towards the lower trail. Hunks of snow came bouncing and flying around him. One hit his chest and almost knocked him out of the saddle. Another smashed into the horse's head and it staggered. Drayton fought it through, standing in the stirrups, arms straining at the reins. Something burst against his shoulders and shrouded the world in streaks of white as it knocked him forward.

Then the horse was going down again and he knew that this time he could never hold it up. He kicked free of the stirrups and a solid wall smashed into him, hurling him downslope as if he had been shot out of a cannon. He cart-wheeled, limbs flailing futilely, the world jerking and swirling out of orbit as he crashed into the slope in the midst of endless, deafening thunder. He stood on his head, was flung on to his back, kicked onto his face, pummelled and rolled, smashed in the midriff and hurled momentarily out into clear air, glimpsing blue sky before the world crashed on top of him in a terrible, tearing violence so that he couldn't breathe. His mouth and nostrils were clogged with snow. He wasn't still for a second, churned and shoved and catapulted downslope, lights exploding behind his eyes, his chest feeling crushed, lungs ready to burst.

Then the lights went out and the whole mountain came down on top of him in an awful, black silence that was as cold as death.

★ ★ ★

There was warmth again. And pain, *lots and lots* of pain. One arm was strapped across his chest, his lower ribs heavily bandaged by the feel of them. He felt other bandages around his right knee and ankle. Hesitantly, he opened his eyes.

An angel hovered over him.

Then he saw that it was Evelyn Bridges and he was in the big cabin that Boy Daniels had used at the Sierra High gold camp. Bedclothes were piled on top of him and a fire blazed in the old hearth.

She told him the snow slide had carried him down right onto the wide ledge as far as the abandoned gold mines. He had been on the very edge of the avalanche when she had found him, half-buried, half-alive. He had been unconscious for three days.

He looked about him. 'Sandy . . . ?'

Evelyn smiled. 'Gone. She's anxious to get to Laramie and take over that whorehouse she was managing for Gunn. She's afraid someone else might beat her to it if she doesn't hurry.'

He nodded slowly. 'Sandy's a survivor . . . no one else made it?'

'No one. Will you go back to Texas now, Buck?'

'Reckon so.'

'You should be able to ride in a few days. What will you tell Mr Daniels about Boy?'

His eyes swung to her. 'That he died a hero's death, trying to save me from Gunn, got caught by the avalanche.'

'*Is* that what happened, Buck?'

'J.D.'ll believe it if I tell him so — and if you were to write a short article for your paper along those lines.'

She was silent briefly, then smiled. 'It'll be one of my last articles. I'm closing the paper. Can't afford a new press.' She looked at him soberly. 'You're really quite a softy at heart, aren't you, Buck Drayton?'

'Maybe it's just that I'm a little scared.'

She was surprised at the admission. 'Of what?'

'Old friend of J.D.'s named Ben Ivo threatened to kill me if I brought back a bad report about Boy.'

'I don't believe you're scared of anything.'

He reached out with his good hand

and touched her arm. 'Scared to ask you to go back to Texas with me.'

She laughed. 'You just did!'

'Well, scared to hear your answer.'

'Afraid I'll say *yes*?'

'Afraid you won't.'

She smiled, shaking her head slightly as she closed one warm, small hand over his on her arm.

'You foolish man, there's no need to be scared at all.'

THE END

We do hope that you have enjoyed reading this large print book.

Did you know that all of our titles are available for purchase?

We publish a wide range of high quality large print books including:
Romances, Mysteries, Classics
General Fiction
Non Fiction and Westerns

Special interest titles available in large print are:
The Little Oxford Dictionary
Music Book, Song Book
Hymn Book, Service Book

Also available from us courtesy of Oxford University Press:
Young Readers' Dictionary
(large print edition)
Young Readers' Thesaurus
(large print edition)

For further information or a free brochure, please contact us at:
Ulverscroft Large Print Books Ltd.,
The Green, Bradgate Road, Anstey,
Leicester, LE7 7FU, England.
Tel: (00 44) **0116 236 4325**
Fax: (00 44) **0116 234 0205**

Other titles in the
Linford Western Library:

STONE MOUNTAIN

Concho Bradley

The stage robbery had been accomplished by an old woman. Twine Fourch had never heard of a female being a highway robber before. He followed the trail all the way to a dilapidated log cabin up Stone Mountain. What happened after that no one could believe even after townsmen from Jefferson found the old log house and the skeletal dying old woman. But before the mystery could be solved there would be two unnecessary killings, a bizarre suicide and a lynching.

GUNS OF THE GAMBLER

M. Duggan

Destitute gambler Ben Crow arrives in Mallory keen to claim his inheritance, only to discover that rancher Edward Bacon has other ideas. Set up by Miss Dorothy, who had fooled him completely, Ben finds himself dangling on the end of a rope. Saved from death, Ben sets off in pursuit of Miss Dorothy, determined upon retribution. However, his quest for vengeance turns into a rescue mission when she is kidnapped by a crazy man-burning bandit.

SIDEWINDER

John Dyson

All Flynn wants is to be Marshal of Tucson, but he is framed by the territory's richest rancher, Frank Buchanan, and thrown into Yuma prison. Five years later Flynn comes out, intent on clearing his name and burning for vengeance. Fists thud, knives flash and bullets fly as he rides both sides of the law and participates in kidnapping and double-dealing. He is once again arrested for a murder of which he is innocent. Can he escape the noose a second time?